Rough Living

Rough Living

Tokuda Shūsei

Translated by Richard Torrance

University of Hawai'i Press
HONOLULU

Originally serialized in Japanese under the title *Arakure* in
Yomiuri Shinbun in 1915

Library of Congress Cataloging-in-Publication Data
Tokuda, Shusei, 1872–1943
  [Arakure. English]
  Rough living / Tokuda Shusei ; translated by Richard Torrance.
     p. cm.
  Includes bibliographical references.
  ISBN 0–8248–2336–2 (cloth : alk. paper) —
ISBN 0–8248–2387–7 (pbk. : alk. paper)
  I. Title.
PL817.O36 A913 2001
895.6'342—dc21

                                                00–049753

This book has been supported in part by a grant from
the College of Humanities and the Office of Research
and Graduate Studies at the Ohio State University.

Designed by Kenneth Miyamoto
Printed by The Maple-Vail Book Manufacturing Group

*This translation is for
my mother, Eileen Torrance*

Contents

Acknowledgments

I WISH TO THANK Professor Edwin McClellan, who first introduced me to this novel and made reading and discussing it a pleasure. Professor Jun Etō, recently deceased, went over this work with me in the original line by line. Jay Rubin and William Tyler read portions of early drafts and offered valuable suggestions. The anonymous readers who reviewed the translation were extraordinarily diligent and helpful. Sharon Yamamoto was unstinting in her support of this project from the beginning to the end. I would also like to thank my wife, Emiko, who endured hours of irritating questions about obscure usages. Needless to say, errors and infelicities are my own. I would also like to thank Chiseo Kimura, who graciously granted permission to use the illustration *Yushima no keidai,* by Kimura Shōhachi, for the cover.

Translator's Introduction

By the time of his death, Tokuda Shūsei (1872–1943) was respected as Japan's most accomplished novelistic chronicler of the urban working class and common life.[1] Kawabata Yasunari (1899–1972), the 1968 Nobel laureate for literature, wrote that Shūsei was a master of the novel, a master who maintained no school and who was the most Japanese of all modern novelists in the sense of being the most closely in touch with his own society. Kawabata also argued that there are three pinnacles in the history of the Japanese novel: Murasaki Shikibu (fl. ca. 1000), Ihara Saikaku (1642–1693), and Tokuda Shūsei.[2] Nakamura Murao stated that, after Saikaku, only Shūsei portrayed the true characteristics of the Japanese people.[3] Takeda Rintarō also saw Shūsei as Ihara Saikaku's modern successor.[4] Murō Saisei, Uno Kōji, Chikamatsu Shūkō, Hirotsu Kazuo, Aono Suekichi, Takami Jun, Kojima Masajirō, Shinoda Hajime, and Etō Jun are among the writers and critics who have expressed admiration of, and even wonder at, Shūsei's mature literature.[5]

By the 1930s, young writers defending freedom of speech and resisting authoritarian political movements had begun to rally around Shūsei. He accepted the chairmanship of the League of Academic and Artistic Freedom, one of the few organizations opposing greater government restriction of the arts and literature at that time. A literary coterie formed around Shūsei and published a journal, *Arakure* (Rough living), devoted to a kind of liberal cosmopolitanism. Writers associated with Japan's version of the popular front, the *Jinmin bunko* (People's library; a literary magazine) group of writers, praised Shūsei as the embodiment of the "Spirit of Prose Literature," a slogan used in the fight against the "poetic neoromanticism" of Japanese

1

fascism. Young writers associated with the Left were arrested for subversive activities when they met under the auspices of the Tokuda Shūsei Study Group.[6] Why Shūsei's mature fiction inspired such respect and controversy is a question that can probably best be approached historically.

Throughout his career as a professional novelist, a career that lasted from about 1895 to 1942, Shūsei remained committed to the egalitarian ideals of the Meiji period. He participated in the people's rights movement in the 1880s and worked at provincial newspapers associated with the Liberal Party, the inheritor of the mantle of the people's rights movement. His earliest published works of fiction, appearing in the mid-1890s and sponsored by the utopian socialist Taoka Reiun (1870–1912), were polemics denouncing the rich and powerful in Japanese society. As will be discussed below, after the Russo-Japanese War (1904–1905), he explored the egalitarian implications of Japanese naturalism. In 1923, Shūsei wrote that he had lived most of his life as a member of the propertyless classes and that he thought that all writers should imbue their works with what he called "the revolutionary spirit." In 1927, Shūsei maintained that, as an individual, he identified more with the proletariat than with any other class.[7] In a 1936 preface to one of his books, he wrote, "This volume reflects my deep interest in the lower classes and my growing conviction that I have lived my life together with the masses."[8] Addressing the war effort in 1942, he wrote, "What we must never forget or ignore is the individual human being. All of us must live first and foremost as human beings."[9]

For Shūsei the novelist, identification with the "masses" was translated into various concepts of realism. At the start of his career, he read and imitated the works of Western realists—Émile Zola, Guy de Maupassant, Charles Dickens, Victor Hugo, and Alphonse Daudet, among others—but, in 1905, he realized that his novels written under their direct influence were "entirely inadequate for the serious representation and analysis of human affairs."[10] Shūsei turned away from Western literary models and explored ways in which to incorporate extraliterary language in his work and circumvent the literary stereotypes inherent in the Japanese literary tradition. The transformation in Shūsei's writing corresponds with the rise of Japanese naturalism in the first decade of the twentieth century and involves experimentation with narrative perspective: how the novelist could allow working-class characters to speak, see, and feel in languages that were true to the character and yet not demeaning or patronizing.[11] Little or no foreign influence can be discerned in his solutions to this problem. As Masamune Hakuchō (1879–1962), one of Japan's most distinguished critics and authors, observed in 1920, "One will almost certainly not find a novelistic style like Shūsei's in a foreign work." In the critic Nakamura Seiko's words, "Shūsei is unique to Japan."[12]

One reason that Shūsei is compared so often to Saikaku, the archetypical figure and originator of Japanese realism, has to do with the distinctive ways that Shūsei discovered to write about lower-class characters. When writing for a popular audience, he adhered to generic conventions in literally hundreds of novels and short stories. In these works, he punished the rich and powerful and sympathetically portrayed the weak and oppressed. On the other hand, he attempted to circumvent generic convention in a series of novels and short stories in which he experimented with ways to narrate the world from the perspectives of common characters. Writers and critics marveled at the seemingly innumerable "tricks" that Shūsei developed to make language of great complexity and beauty "belong to" his characters, who were generally not very articulate. It was this latter Shūsei who came to be recognized as one of Japan's most original and talented novelists. In truth, however, one Shūsei was the mirror image of the other.

Shūsei the popular writer was the product of an apprenticeship starting in 1895 to Ozaki Kōyō (1897–1903), the most easily marketed writer of the day and the founder of several guilds that promoted and protected novelists in the midst of one of the most remarkable publishing booms in the history of the world. Through the intermediation of Izumi Kyōka (1873–1939), a fellow Kanazawa native, Shūsei became a live-in student of the craft of the novel in a "school"/dormitory in the back of Ozaki Kōyō's house. He remained associated with Kōyō's stable of writers until Kōyō's death in 1903—and, in the public's mind, until after the Russo-Japanese War.

His association with Kōyō's school taught Shūsei a great deal about the fictional techniques and the vocabulary of the classical tradition as it was being updated and adapted to modern melodrama. Under Kōyō, Shūsei also learned how to write quickly and how to write for different audiences. From 1895 to 1915, he produced approximately 285 short stories and novellas, 16 children's stories, 22 translations, 110 haiku, 44 long serialized novels for a popular audience, and 5 major novels that have since been acclaimed as masterpieces of Japanese naturalism. He tended to publish his writing in periodicals with readerships appropriate to the literary work in question. He serialized his major novels in newspapers with a substantial urban circulation, newspapers such as *Yomiuri*, *Asahi*, and *Kokumin shinbun*. More popular works were sent to provincial papers distant from the central literary world in Tokyo, some as far away as Korea and Manchuria. Short stories were often commissioned by magazines with connections to Ozaki's guild, including in 1898 and 1899, for example, *Shōnen bunshū* (Collected young people's writings), *Shinshōsetsu* (The new novel), Shun'yōdō's journal for a popular readership, *Jogaku kōgi* (Lectures for young ladies), *Joshi no tomo* (The young lady's friend), and *Bungei kurabu* (Literary club), Hakubunkan's literary journal for a popular readership. Other short stories were written specifically for journals with an intellectual readership: *Shinchō* (The new tide), *Chūō kōron* (Central review), and, later, *Kaizō* (Reconstruction) and *Bungei shunjū* (Spring and autumn literary arts).[13]

Among the members of Kōyō's guild, Shūsei was a different presence. He took political issues more seriously. His fiction concerned class conflict, women's rights and the emergence of the new independent woman, and discrimination against *eta* (a class of outcasts within Japanese society), themes that were dealt with much later in Japan by such writers as Shimazaki Tōson (1872–1943) and Arishima Takeo (1878–1923).[14] Better educated than other members of the guild, and also able to read English, Shūsei introduced the group to works of Western literature. From the first, he was the realist of the guild, and, after Ozaki's death in 1903, while other members of the guild polished and transformed formulas inherited from the past, reworking them for a popular audience (sometimes brilliantly), Shūsei incorporated stylistic innovations from the sketch-from-life movement (the "haikuesque" prose movement advocated by Takahama Kyoshi) in his work and met head-on the challenge of naturalism. He was the only one of Kōyō's disciples to survive as a professional realist novelist into the second decade of the twentieth century. However, in the end, the reason that "the respected Shūsei," the literary innovator, could break so many of the rules of linear narrative development is because he had mastered the conventions of popular fiction.

Tokuda Shūsei and Japanese Naturalism

In Japanese literary histories, Tokuda Shūsei is most often held to personify Japanese naturalism. Whether this association is justified depends on how one defines *naturalism*. If one traces the ideological genealogy of Japanese naturalism from a Western-inspired Christian Romanticism that influenced Kitamura Tōkoku (1868–1894), Shimazaki Tōson, Kunikida Doppo (1871–1908), and Masamune Hakuchō with its emphasis, derived from such varied sources as the Bible and William Wordsworth, on platonic love, confession, and the discovery of the self, then Shūsei was definitely not a part of the movement. Or, if one considers naturalism to be a new set of materialistic beliefs more amenable than an earlier conception of realism *(shajitsu)* to the idea that instinctual motives—bestial sexual desires, racial or hereditary proclivities, or innate aggression—determine human behavior, then Shūsei was only superficially a "naturalist" in a few of his more conceptually realistic works for a popular audience. The association of Shūsei with naturalism is probably justified, however, if one understands naturalism as Shūsei himself characterized it in 1942:

> At about the time of the Russo-Japanese War, the nation's citizens entered a whole new stage of self-awareness, and the new literary trends dominated as a surging tide. It was not limited to naturalism, for which Tayama Katai and others propagandized so passionately; by reacting critically to naturalism, other writers as well helped create the new literature. I do not know whether the naturalism of Tayama Katai and the others was truly grounded in French naturalism, but, whether it was or not, as realism it represented enormous progress in the way in which people were perceived and portrayed when compared to the so-called *shajitsu* form of realism that preceded it. . . . It was during this period that the Japanese people, who for generations had been kept subservient, cast off their fetters and awakened to their humanity.[15]

As Japan's first mass literary movement, naturalism encouraged more people (including large numbers of students) to write in a realist style than ever before, revolutionized the subject matter of literature, and transformed Japanese literary stylistics. It provided novelists with the theoretical justification that allowed them to portray ordinary individuals participating in the creation of history. Through literary characterization, the life of an ordinary person could serve as a microcosm of the past and future of the nation. This is true in the case of Tayama Katai's *Inaka kyōshi* (1909), Shimazaki Tōson's *Yoake-mae* (1929–1935), and much of Shūsei's work.[16]

Shūsei brought ideas imported from the West by members of the educated elite down to the level of ordinary Japanese men and women, where they took on new significance. While *individualism (kojin-shugi)* was generally used in the Meiji era to denote a liberal intellectual discourse advocating rationality and independence from family and tradition, in his *Arajotai* (The new household, 1908) Shūsei applied the concept to the life of a sake merchant who is struggling to establish a shop in an impoverished neighborhood. This "individualism" is a loneliness caused by the economic necessities of capitalism, an alienation far more common than the angst of intellectuals. The "independent household" *(katei)* of the newly emerging nuclear family became in *Tadare* (Festering, 1913) the sensual, decadent realm of an ex-prostitute and her prosperous but slightly crooked husband. "The new woman" became in *Ashiato* (Footprints, 1910) and *Arakure* (Rough living, 1915) the next-door maid or the independent businesswoman, a woman who would not endure the indignities of a traditional marriage, the sex trades, or the apprenticeship system. Perhaps most crucially, if the reader were to be transported across class and gender lines and thrust into complex new sociolinguistic realms being explored by novelists with an interest in common life as a source of beauty and the determinant of Japan's future, then the prevailing generic codes marking characters as members of the lower classes or as disreputable women had to be radically disrupted.

This, I think, is one reason for the unique temporal structures of Shūsei's best work. The "plot," if it can be called that, progresses according to declarative sentences. The reader is then taken back into the past through a series of associations both within and beyond the character's memory—that peculiarity of language in the novel that consists of the layering of consciousnesses, what Bakhtin has called "novelistic hybridization"[17]—that eventually return to the narrative present, at which point the process starts over. This technique foregrounds everyday conscious time at the expense of dramatic time. The author is free to incorporate literary and extraliterary language in the consciousness of common characters. The resulting memories within memories, at times crystallizing in present moments of naturalistic impressionism, portray the literary nature of consciousness in the ways in which human beings perceive the world: it does not matter whether the character is barely literate or not very articulate; in the end, he or she interprets experience according to complex literary paradigms.

The major naturalistic novels that Shūsei completed between 1908 and 1915 were all based on stories that he "picked up" at home or within a twenty-minute walk of his house in the Morikawa district of Tokyo's Hongō ward. The daily experience of the wine merchant across the street from where he once lived became the basis of the novel *Arajotai;* the life of the next-door maid, later his wife, and his first years of marriage to her provided the material for *Ashiato* and *Kabi* (Mold, 1911); the career of a former prostitute, his wife's friend, became the subject of *Tadare.* His treatment of these materials was in absolute contrast to his former writing as "the Western-influenced realist" under Ozaki Kōyō. He probably stopped reading foreign literature altogether, and, in his best writing, there is no discernible Western influence. When he had a documentary source, a living model, for his fiction, it was as if he felt the need to reinvent the novel to account for this randomly found human situation; otherwise, he tended to work within established genres. He understood only too well the temptation to surrender to the conventions of popular entertainment and the difficulties of creating innovative fiction, of "making it new," for, as he instructed young writers in 1913, "You must work, as a human being and as an author, to avoid being caught by form. It is so easy to get caught."[18] He spoke from experience.

For much of his forty-five-year literary career, Shūsei managed to earn a living as a professional novelist—raise a large family of, at times, eight dependents, educate his children, buy a house, and so on—by observing a dichotomy in his writing. He maintained his reputation as a serious writer by working in an experimental mode of realism, producing work that was often critically well received, and then using that reputation to sell popular works of what might be called *conceptual realism*—for example, melodrama, mystery fiction, novels of the demimonde—for serialized publication in periodicals considered to have a less than discriminating readership. *Arakure* (1915), translated here as *Rough Living,* represents the tendency in his work toward an experimental mode of realism.

Rough Living

Shūsei's *Arakure* concerns a seamstress named Oshima, a character based on Suzuki Chiyo, Shūsei's sister-in-law. The novel was serialized daily in the newspaper *Yomiuri shinbun* from January to July 1915 and was published as a book in September 1915. It was almost universally praised as the most substantial work of fiction of the year.[19] Nonetheless, in an October 1915 interview, Shūsei stated that, while he could write two or three more novels like *Arakure* were he so inclined, he was tired of "that kind of thing" and did not intend to write other works like it. He was true to his word. *Arakure* is the last of his major novels of common life set in the Meiji period.

Donald Keene has translated the title of this novel as "The Wild One." This may be closer to Shūsei's original intention. In 1915, Shūsei wrote:

> I first intended to title *Arakure Yajū no gotoku* [Like a wild beast], but, when I was about to start writing, I changed it. I had come up with some very imaginative fictionalizations for that material. I was trying to portray a modern type with extremely rough nerves . . . a person who paid absolutely no heed to the social conventions of duty and civility [*giri-ninjō*] and who was ceaselessly compelled to action. One does not often encounter such people in real life. But, owing to all the petty irritations that I was experiencing at the time, I felt a great attraction to just such a person, and the woman who was the model for the protagonist of the work was a person with some of those same tendencies. To put it bluntly, I intended to re-create that woman as my ideal. When I actually started writing, however, I succeeded in only a few respects. I drew away from the novel that I had started to write and found myself adhering too closely to reality.[20]

However, "The Wild Woman," "The Tempest," "The Outlaw," "The Ruffian," or similar translations of the title invoke the Western theatrical and cinematic tradition, leaving the reader with inappropriate expectations. On the other hand, if Shūsei had intended the nominal form of the verb *arakureru* (rough, wild) as only a concrete noun referring to a specific person, he might have indicated this by adding a suffix: *arakure-mono* (ruffian) or *arakure-onna* (rough woman). The title that Shūsei ultimately chose allows the semantic space to translate the noun in a more abstract sense, as a "life" and a "way of living." "Rough living" is a fairly accurate description of the contents of the novel, tones down Shūsei's originally conceived title, and remains within the semantic scope of the nominalized form of the Japanese verb *arakureru* in the sense of *arakureta seikatsu* (a rough life).

Rough Living is, in some respects, Shūsei's least technically accomplished and innovative serious novel of the period from 1907 to 1915. It lacks the severe and insightful sociological summings-up of *Arajotai*. Narrative perspective tends to drift away from the protagonist, as it does not in *Ashiato*. In all Shūsei's serious work, time is that of everyday consciousness—digression, memory, and association—but the temporal structure of *Rough Living* is not nearly as complex as that of *Kabi,* in which past and present can barely be distinguished. Finally, while *Rough Living* deals quite frankly with sexuality and sexual dysfunction and was quite shocking to many readers at the time it first appeared, it does not provide the sort of erotic charge to be found in *Tadare.*

Nonetheless, *Rough Living* remains Shūsei's representative work. It is his most accessible and popular novel because of the humor, exuberance, and spirit of rebellion personified by its protagonist, Oshima. Through Oshima's eyes, we see the formation of the structures underlying everyday life in a modern capitalist society as they were evolving in Japan from the time of Oshima's birth in 1884 until the end of the novel in about 1910. Portrayed as it is coming into existence in Japan, modern capitalism seems invigorated, enormously liberating, enriching people more than it impoverishes, and creating the tragic denouements of a lifetime every week and a half or so.

As a product of this new social order, Oshima herself is independent and indomitable. Her response to adversity is to fight her way past whatever obstacles fate has thrown in her path, taking great delight in the various strategies that she develops. Readers probably derive vicarious pleasure from the sheer joy that Oshima takes in her physicality. Relatively petty disappointments often bring about depression and pain, but, in moments of real crisis, she rises to the occasion with assurance and physical vitality. The humor in the novel also derives in part from self-recognition on the part of Oshima and the reader rather than from comic stereotyping. Oshima is often laughing, chuckling, or smiling, and such a response represents an awareness of the incongruity inherent in her position or a given social situation. This incongruity arises in part from the disparity between the ideological certainty with which those in authority speak and the irrelevance of their words in the light of reality. If an older person in authority makes a pronouncement, it is almost certainly self-serving or wrong. There are frequent reversals of gender roles. Men often do the cooking and flower arranging, and women issue commands and work outside the home.

Of all Shūsei's remarkable heroines, Oshima invites the broadest sense of familiarity and identification on the part of a mass readership. While Oshima may have been a new type of woman in her day, she is not a new type any longer. The typical Japanese reader today sees Oshimas all around, and the character comes alive as a touchstone or standard by which present-day Japanese society can be judged or measured. This is because certain aspects of Japanese culture and society have remained constant over the years. In what follows, certain of those aspects will be briefly examined: the diminished authority of folklore; the improving status of women; the currency of the success ethic; the longing for romance; the importance of festivals; and the Westernization of popular manners, fashion, and customs.

From the child Oshima's perspective, we are introduced to a series of folkloric associations, associations that give rise to certain expectations that are then frustrated. For example, one expects the ill treatment of children at the hands of an "evil stepmother," but it is Oshima's real mother who has formed an obsessive hatred of her. Oshima's foster mother at first appears kind and compassionate, but even she turns out to be as deceptive and greedy as any other authority figure in the novel. The ferry crossing at Ogu on the banks of the Sumida river, traditionally associated with the kidnapping, enslavement, murder, and abandonment of children, should be the site of a similar tragedy for Oshima; instead, expectations are undercut, and, through the intermediation of Nishida, Oshima is adopted by a prosperous family.[21] The wealth of Oshima's foster parents in turn brings to mind other folktales, particularly the story—common during the Meiji period—of the wandering monk (*rokubu*) bearing a Buddhist altar on his back who begs for a night's lodging and is robbed and murdered by his hosts. Thus, the story of the monk's death that Oshima's friends tell at school is as much a "fairy tale" as her foster father's version. While the belief that the soul of the vengeful monk returns to strike blind the offspring of his murderers is occasionally of some concern to Oshima, her negligence in not receiving the "holy waters" at the temple Nishi-Arai Daishi—instead she drinks a bottle of soda—indicates that she is able to ignore superstition with few ill effects.[22]

By 1900, Ōji Paper Manufacturing, which would become one of the largest producers of paper in Japan, has expanded and built a huge new factory in Ōji, effectively marginalizing smaller craftsmen, such as Oshima's foster parents. The indirect result is the kind of capitalization of the countryside that the foster parents profit from and that breeds local resentment in the form of tales of murdered Buddhist monks who curse the ill-gotten gains of the newly prosperous. The authority of myth, Confucian morality, and feudal custom is undercut by the greater opportunities available to Oshima's generation. Oshima emerges from feudalism to define herself rationally, independent of family and community and tales of their origin. She refuses to act like a character in a play or a popular novel. She is, in short, a modern individual.

This brings us to the subject of the status of women in Meiji society. According to the Meiji civil code, women had almost no rights under the law. Based on Confucian concepts of the proper role of women, the law held that, in all social situations, women were to be subservient to men: first to their fathers, then to their husbands, and, finally, to their sons. The ideal woman, championed by government officials, especially those associated with the Ministry of Education, was the "good wife, wise mother" *(ryōsai kenbo)*, whose proper field of activity was to be limited to her nurturing, supportive, and subservient role within the household *(ie)*. One cannot help but note that these legal and semilegal abstractions have little currency in or relevance to Oshima's world. Women's rights and status are protected by common custom, which directly contradicts official legal provisions.

Women had no legal right to inherit property, for example, but common custom in *Rough Living* seems to indicate that Oshima's sister (and her husband) has a substantial inheritance coming. True, Oshima is disinherited, but this is her mother's doing, one woman's misguided whim, not the heavy hand of tradition. Oshima would appear to be the exception that proves the rule of the daughter's right to inherit. The law also gave women no rights in divorce proceedings, but, in the world that Shūsei portrays, men must pay substantial amounts to separate, not only from wives, but also from mistresses, and even from lovers.[23] Although the notion of women functioning as heads of households was anathema to a state ideology that defined the nation as one great family with a male emperor at its head, in the novel women take over as effective heads of households as a matter of course—for example, the old woman at Uegen, who is firmly in control of her household, and the woman owner of the hot-spring resort to which Oshima is sent after she begins an affair with the innkeeper in Shiobara. The possibility is even advanced that Oshima will take over her father's business, a possibility that is foreclosed when she leaves for the mountains with her brother. Oshima's independence is, in part, made possible by traditional common custom as it evolves to deal with modern times.[24] The nation's legal system—patterned on Western models—is largely absent or irrelevant in Oshima's world.

Almost all historical treatments of the "ethic of success" (risshin shusse) in the Meiji period ignore women. However, even a cursory reading of Shūsei's novels reveals how important various conceptions of success were to both sexes in Meiji common life. In Rough Living, Oshima is intent on taking advantage of the transformations that Japan is undergoing at about the turn of the century—industrialization, the decline of an older landowning class, imperialistic expansion abroad, and the Westernization of native customs and manners. These transformations are disassembled and reconstituted in Oshima's field of vision and are generally felt as different perceptions of time. In chapters 1–61, time passes according to the natural progression of the seasons. Although, in the first decade of the twentieth century, Ōji and Ogu are in the process of losing their agricultural character as they gradually become suburbs of Tokyo, the local economy is still dependent on cyclic, seasonal fluctuations in supply and demand. Scenes of natural beauty in changing seasonal aspect, a leisurely pace of life, and a feeling of being confined or trapped often dominate Oshima's perceptions. Similarly, the urban district of Kanda remains the realm of an older Edo bourgeoisie, a class that has almost disappeared today and is shown in precipitous decline in the novel. During her sojourn deep in the mountains, Oshima is immersed in dead time, a function of a primary economy dependent on mining, sericulture (silk being at that time Japan's primary export), and tourism.

With Oshima's return to the city in 1904, the nature of temporal change has been transfigured. From chapter 62 on, time is no longer anchored in agriculture and the cycles of nature and is now determined by external institutional and political agendas: the Russo-Japanese War, the 1907 Exhibition of Industry and Commerce, and the academic year of the public school system. Oshima's motives seem clear enough in making the transition to a nonseasonal, fully capitalistic economy. Economic success is, after all, her only means of maintaining common respectability, which she comes perilously close to losing. Her contempt for prostitutes, other workers in the sex trades of the demimonde, landless peasants with "the despicable character of a slave" (p. 46), and workmen is an expression of her resolve not to fall out of the realm of common respectability. Further, her desire for success is motivated by a desire for revenge. She is born into a situation in which the deck is stacked against her, and, in creating her own fortune against all odds, she defies the strictures of the past. Oshima is the hero of an age that is still with us. In sensing in cityscapes the direction of consumer desire and wagering everything again and again on her hunches, she personifies that hungry, entrepreneurial spirit of "the free individual" who has no place in the traditional order, a spirit that represents an extraordinary challenge to novelistic articulation because it in turn defies most rules of genre.

But what does Oshima really want? At one point, she thinks that all her striving for success represents merely the sublimation of other, more shadowy desires, and, as soon as she gains some measure of success and security, she plans to give it all up. Perhaps readers identify with Oshima's ambivalence. The objects of her yearning are by their nature ephemeral. But there is also a universality in her longing for love and affection. Achieving success is a highly addictive game that coarsens Oshima's personality and her capacity for sympathy, yet it does not seem to diminish her sexual generosity or her willingness to sacrifice for romance with little expectation of material gain. Desire moves Oshima to transcend economics.

Oshima loves novelty and fun, and life in the city seems to consist of endless festivals and the exoticism of the new. The two most important celebrations of the year are the Festival of Souls *(obon)* in mid-July and the New Year's festivities *(shōgatsu)*. These are also the critical deadlines in the business year. It is the custom in common life that, if one can pay off one's debts by these holidays, credit is extended through the coming year. If one cannot pay off one's debts, credit is not extended further, and, especially for a business like that of the tailor, bankruptcy almost inevitably results. The Festival of Souls, when households welcome home the souls of ancestors, is traditionally the holiday when servants are allowed to visit their families, and it provides Oshima the opportunity to stay in touch with her natural family. In addition, there are the countless local festivals and activities in entertainment districts like Asakusa and neighborhoods around temples and shrines that offered diversions for men and women on a daily basis. And, of course, Oshima's world is shot through with reference to prostitutes and semiprostitutes, whose fashions and manners influence the world of the commonly respectable.

The opportunities for success afforded Oshima generally have to do with the growth of a utilitarian mass culture heavily influenced by Western fashions and entertainments. Such fashions and amusements are generally portrayed in the novel as superficial: Onoda's phonograph or Oshima's declaration that her Western-style dress is for work and that she does not care how she looks. However, these manifestations of the West (the West as it influenced the majority of the population in Japan) reveal significant changes. The demand for Western-style clothing undoubtedly came about because of the literal "uniforming" of Japanese society at around the time of the Russo-Japanese War: military uniforms for officers and soldiers; uniforms for postmen, railroad conductors, and policemen; court dress; tuxedos and morning coats worn at upper-class social events; the frock coats worn by politicians, educators, and doctors; and uniforms for the small percentage of students who made it to middle school and beyond. At least in Tokyo, the distinction between public and private clothing for men—Western-style clothing for official occasions and government employment, Japanese-style clothing for use at home and for personal ceremonies—appears to have been well established in the years after the Russo-Japanese War. [25]

The Westernization of popular customs and manners in everyday life can be attributed to the utility of Western fashion, and the value placed on utility owed a great deal in turn to the militarization of the Japanese economy as a whole, or at least civilian spinoffs from the military. Of course, Oshima benefits enormously from these trends. Indeed, one begins to see "internationalization" in terms of the sexual attraction of this utility: from Oshima's perspective, Western men's clothing symbolizes vigor and strength, while traditional clothing is held to represent the effeminate.

Problems of Translation

As was suggested above, in Shūsei's serious novels, the voice of the author is refracted through an enormous diversity of languages: highly original sound symbolism (conventionally held to be not literary), the representation of regional and urban dialects, nonstandard pseudoclassical narrative forms, beautiful seasonal imagery, and dialogue in mixed dialects. These features make his works difficult to translate.

At times, the voice of the narrator seems an invisible mediator, simply presenting Oshima's/Suzuki Chiyo's words. At other times, it seems an objective, documentary presence narrating the events of Oshima's life and the entertaining backgrounds of the host of eccentric characters who appear and disappear in the course of the novel. Frequently, there is the pure stylist in the tradition of Japanese nature description, yet we also glimpse the radical modernist, constructing flashbacks and digressions within digressions, all within Oshima's consciousness. The varying tones and narrative techniques again make for difficult translation.

All Shūsei's serious novels were written for daily serialization in newspapers. Because Shūsei used the features of serialization as an integral part of the structure of *Rough Living,* I have retained in translation the chapter numbers, which reflect the divisions imposed by daily serialization. In his serious fiction, Shūsei showed little concern for maintaining tension or suspense in the plot, believing that page-turning plots (and Western ideas) were more appropriate for a popular audience. There is no evidence that he was influenced, as were some authors at the time, by letters to the editor voicing complaints or suggesting revisions or future plot developments.[26] As was previously indicated, he would often "give away" the conclusion of his story at the start of a day's serialization and then depend on the strength of his literary technique to keep the reader interested until he had "caught up" with his conclusion.

An example of this sort of "inverted narration" is found at the start of chapter 18, which opens: "The second time that Oshima ran away from her foster family was just after her wedding to Saku, toward the end of autumn of the same year" (p. 48). The narrative does not catch up with the narrative present—toward the end of autumn 1901, when Oshima runs away—until chapter 23. Yet a close reading and "unraveling" of the complicated temporal structure of the work reveals that it is all perfectly consistent, and every major incident in the book can be fairly consistently dated. A chronology of events in the novel appears in the appendix.

The effect of the work as a whole in Japanese is profoundly humanistic, especially in the treatment of Oshima's childhood. Aesthetic, ideological, or poetic unity cannot be found in Shūsei's best work. On the other hand, what can be found in the original is some intimation, perhaps more than in other literary texts, of the enormous language diversity and complexity that washes over and penetrates most human beings at any given moment. Suffice it to say in conclusion that Oshima's story is one that I want to present in English, however inadequate the translation may be to the original, because her Japan is one that I recognize and identify with and because her life probably remains, even today, not so far distant from the lives of a great many people struggling to find some measure of happiness in the city.

The text translated was taken from volume 4 of *Shūsei zenshū* ([Complete works of Shūsei], 18 vols. [Kyoto: Rinsen Shoten, 1974–1975; reprint, Kyoto: Rinsen Shoten, 1989–1991]), with reference to the recent edition in volume 10 of *Tokuda Shūsei zenshū* ([Complete works of Tokuda Shūsei], 12 vols. to date [Tokyo: Yagi Shoten, 1997–]) and editions in *Tokuda Shūsei shū* ([Tokuda Shūsei anthology], vol. 68 of *Meiji bungaku zenshū* [Tokyo: Chikuma Shobō, 1971]), *Tokuda Shūsei* (vol. 8 of *Nihon bungaku zenshū* [Tokyo: Shūeisha, 1974]), and *Tokuda Shūsei* (vol. 9 of *Nihon bungaku* [Tokyo: Chūō Kōronsha, 1973]).[27]

Notes

1. Tokuda Shūsei was born Tokuda Sueo to a respectable *bushi* or samurai family who were retainers of the Yokoyama house in the Kaga domain, present-day Ishikawa prefecture. The *bushi* or gentry population of the domainal capital, Kanazawa, was particularly hard hit by the changes brought about by the Meiji

Restoration of 1868, when the hereditary *bushi* class was deprived of its social status, and Shūsei's memories of his youth are colored by poverty and the social chaos caused by such large-scale loss of status. He entered what would become the Fourth Higher School but dropped out of this elite educational track in 1891 owing to poor grades and a lack of money. After stints at provincial newspapers, Shūsei found a niche in the central literary world in Tokyo and supported himself as a professional novelist from about 1895 until his death in 1943.

2. Kawabata Yasunari, "Kaisetsu," in *Tokuda Shūsei shū I*, vol. 9 of *Nihon no bungaku* (Tokyo: Chūō Kōron, 1973), 519–520; and as quoted in Kōno Toshirō, "Hibonkaku-han *Shūsei zenshū* no 'Naiyō mihon' to 'Geppō,'" in *Ronkō Tokuda Shūsei*, ed. Kōno Toshirō (Tokyo: Ōfūsha, 1982), 248–249.

3. Nakamura Murao quoted in Kōno, "Hibonkaku-han *Shūsei zenshū* no 'Naiyō mihon' to 'Geppō,'" 247.

4. Takami Jun, Takeda Rintarō, Hirotsu Kazuo, and Tokuda Shūsei, "Sanbun-seishin o kiku" (a roundtable discussion), *Jinmin bunko* 1, no. 9 (November 1936): 80–91; and Ōtani Kōichi, *Hyōden Takeda Rintarō* (Tokyo: Kawade Shobō Shinsha, 1982), 200, 380–385, 390.

5. See Murō Saisei, quoted in Kōno, "Hibonkaku-han *Shūsei zenshū* no 'Naiyō mihon' to 'Geppō,'" 248; Uno Kōji and Hirotsu Kazuo, "Shūsei o kataru" (a roundtable discussion), in "Tokuda Shūsei: Hito to bungaku," a special issue of *Geirin kanpo*, November 1947, 48–58; Uno Kōji, "Bungei jihyō: Shōsetsu no sho-mondai," *Shinchō* 23, no. 5 (May 1926): 22–32; Chikamatsu Shūkō, "Hito oyobi geijutsuka to shite no Tokuda Shūsei-shi," in *Tokuda Shūsei shū*, vol. 68 of *Meiji bungaku zenshū*, (Tokyo: Chikuma Shobō, 1971), 365–370; Hirotsu Kazuo, *Hirotsu Kazuo zenshū*, 12 vols. (Tokyo: Chūō Kōronsha, 1974), 9:186–188; Aono Suekichi, quoted in Kōno, "Hibonkaku-han *Shūsei zenshū* no 'Naiyō mihon' to 'Geppō,'" 248; Takami Jun, "Shūsei bungaku ni kanren shite," *Geirin kanpo*, November 1947, 27–30; Kojima Masajirō, "Shōsetsu no kamisama," *Nihon bungaku zenshū geppō* (Shūeisha) 67 (August 1974): 1–12; Shinoda Hajime, *Nihon no gendai shōsetsu* (Tokyo: Shūeisha, 1980), 236; and Etō Jun, "Tokuda Shūsei to 'jūjitsu shita kanji,'" *Gunzō* 45, no. 3 (March 1990): 172–182.

6. Muramatsu Takeshi et al., eds., *Shōwa hihyō taikei*, 5 vols. (Tokyo: Banchō Shobō, 1968), 2:414–423, 546. Takami Jun, *Shōwa bungaku seisuishi*, 2 vols. (Tokyo: Bungei Shunjūsha, 1958), 2:65–77. On the Tokuda Shūsei Study Group, see Ōtani Kōichi, *Hyōden Takeda Rintarō* (Tokyo: Kawade Shobō, 1982), 241–242.

7. Tokuda Shūsei, "Sakka wa kakumei kibun o motsu," *Shinchō* 30, no. 2 (February 1923): 25–27, and "Gappyō: Shūsei-shi no ren'ai," *Shinchō* 24, no. 10 (October 1927): 127–128. See also Tokuda Shūsei, "Gappyō," *Shinchō* 23, no. 7 (July 1926): 23.

8. Tokuda Shūsei, "Jo ni kaete," in *Kunshō* (Tokyo: Chūō Kōronsha, 1936), 2–3.

9. Tokuda Shūsei, "*Sōwa* shuppan ni nozomite no sakusha no kotoba," in *Sōwa* (Tokyo: Sakurai Shoten, 1942), 2 (located at the end of the volume).

10. Tokuda Shūsei, "Jijo," in *Shōkazoku* (Tokyo: Shun'yōdō, 1905), n.p. (two pages, unpaginated).

11. A fuller and more technical treatment of the development of Shūsei's

stylistics is provided in Richard Torrance, "Tokuda Shūsei and the Representation of *Shomin* Life" (Ph.D. diss., Yale University, 1989), 68–132. See also Richard Torrance, "Bungaku kyōzai toshite no Tokuda Shūsei," *Kokugo kyōiku ronsō* (Shimane Daigaku Kyōiku Gakubu Kokubun Gakkai) 4 (1994): 127–134.

12. Masamune Hakuchō and Nakamura Seiko, "Katai Shūsei ryōshi ni," *Bunshō sekai* 15, no. 11 (November 1920): 126 and 135, respectively.

13. Matsumoto Tōru, "Tokuda Shūsei no chosaku shoshutsu nenpū kō," *Kinki daigaku kyōyōbu kenkyū kiyō* 13, no. 3 (1982): 1–35.

14. See, e.g., "Yabukōji" (Spearflower, 1896), *Kumo no yukue* (Where the clouds go, 1900), and *Shunkō* (Spring light, 1902), in vol. 1 of Tokuda Shūsei, *Shūsei zenshū* (Complete works of Shūsei), 18 vols. (Kyoto: Rinsen Shoten, 1974–1975).

15. Tokuda Shūsei, preface to *Meiji bungaku sakka ron* (Discourse on the novelists of the Meiji period, 1942), reprinted in Tokuda Shūsei, *Kan no bara* (Tokyo: Shuppan Kubashiki Kaisha, 1948), 19–20.

16. For translations, see Tayama Katai, *Country Teacher: A Novel*, trans. Kenneth Henshall (Honolulu: University of Hawai'i Press, 1984); and Shimazaki Tōson, *Before the Dawn*, trans. William E. Naff (Honolulu: University of Hawai'i Press, 1987).

17. Mikhail M. Bakhtin, *The Dialogic Imagination*, trans. Caryl Emerson and Michael Holquist (Austin: University of Texas Press, 1981), 302–311, 358–362.

18. Shūsei as quoted in Enomoto Takashi, "Shūsei bungaku ron II," in "Tokuda Shūsei kenkyū go," a special issue of *Bunshō kurabu*, September 1952, 15. Shūsei made several similar declarations (see, e.g., Tokuda Shūsei, *Shōsetsu no tsukurikata* [Tokyo: Shinchōsha, 1918], 82).

19. See, e.g., Nakamura Seiko, Nogami Shirakawa, and Sōma Gyofū, "*Arakure* no hihyō," *Shinchō* 23, no. 4 (October 1915): 102–105; Kisha (literary reporter), "*Arakure,*" *Waseda bungaku*, October 1915, 8–9; and Kisha (literary reporter), "*Arakure,*" *Bunshō sekai* 10, no. 12 (November 1915): 222–231; Okada Hachiyo, "*Arakure* no Oshima," *Shinchō* 23, no. 5 (November 1915): 82; A.B.C., "Shūsei no geijutsu," *Shinchō* 23, no. 5 (November 1915): 36–39; and Chikamatsu Shūkō, "Shūsei-shi no sakufū," *Bunshō sekai* 11, no. 6 (June 1916): 58–63.

20. Shūsei as quoted in Noguchi Fujio, *Tokuda Shūsei den* (Tokyo: Chikuma Shobō, 1965), 404.

21. The first association that springs to mind is the Umewakamaru legend in the No play *Sumidagawa*, but there must be any number of variations on similar legends, including the *jiuta* (ballad) version of *Sumidagawa*, the version contained in the *Sumidagawa Umewaka engi*, the version in the *Sumidagawa kagami ikeden*, the Tokiwazu variation *Sumidagawa tsuki no koto no ha*, or Kyokutei Bakin's *Sumidagawa bairyū shinsho*. For a perceptive discussion of the mythical elements in *Arakure*, see Ōsugi Shigeo, "*Arakure* ron," *Gunzō* 40, no. 6 (June 1993): 94–130.

22. Ōsugi, "*Arakure* ron," 100–107.

23. Even Okana, the mistress of a mining engineer, receives a separation payment, despite the fact that she has continued to carry on an affair with Oshima's brother, Sōtarō, after Sōtarō has been paid by the engineer to give her up.

24. Shūsei's treatment of women's rights in common custom in *Arakure* is consistent with his treatment of women in his other works (see Richard Torrance, *The Fiction of Tokuda Shūsei and the Emergence of Japan's New Middle Class* [Seattle: University of Washington Press, 1994], 93–95, 166).

25. Shōwa Joshi Daigaku Hifukugaku Kenkyushitsu, ed., *Kindai Nihon fukusōshi* (Tokyo: Kindai Bunka Kenkyūjo, 1971), 115–116. Of course, the spread of Western-style clothing was generally limited to men's clothing (see pp. 314–315).

26. Naitō Hisako, "*Arakure* ron: *Yomiuri fujin furoku* o hojosen ni," *Bungei to hihyō* 8, no. 9 (May 1999): 27. Naitō notes that, although there is no direct evidence of readers' reactions influencing the novel, there may be indirect influence in the form of the "tenor of the times" crystallized in reports on the "new independent woman" in the newly created "women's supplement to the newspaper *Yomiuri*.

27. Readers with a further interest in Tokuda Shūsei, his position in Ozaki Kōyō's guild, or the historical issues raised by the novel should see my *Fiction of Tokuda Shūsei;* Donald Keene, *Dawn to the West: Japanese Literature in the Modern Era, Fiction* (New York: Henry Holt, 1984), 271–281; Charles Inouye, *The Similitude of Blossoms: A Critical Biography of Izumi Kyōka (1873–1939), Japanese Novelist and Playwright* (Cambridge, Mass.: Harvard University Asia Center, 1998); James Fujii, *Complicit Fictions: The Subject in the Modern Japanese Prose Narrative* (Berkeley and Los Angeles: University of California Press, 1993); and Carol Gluck, *Japan's Modern Myths: Ideology in the Late Meiji Period* (Princeton, N.J.: Princeton University Press, 1985).

Rough Living

1

OSHIMA DID NOT KNOW what to think when she first heard hints from her foster parents, the Mizushimas, that they intended to marry her soon to a young man whom they would then adopt as their son and heir.

The seventeen-year-old Oshima was developing a reputation in the neighborhood as a young woman who hated men. Even with her growing notoriety, if only she had behaved like other respectable young women in town and taken up feminine pursuits like sewing or music lessons on the koto, her foster family's wealth would have ensured her standing in local society as an attractive young woman with excellent marriage prospects. But Oshima was not born with such natural grace and dexterity. She hated to sit still in a room, so from an early age she had gone out to work in the fields and paddies, planting and harvesting rice alongside the young men. Indeed, she came to believe that physical labor might suit her better than the tasks traditionally assigned to young ladies. During the season for silkworm raising, she worked harder than anyone in her house. She found her greatest satisfaction in earning praise from her foster parents. She was often teased in a lewd manner by the young men and hired laborers she worked with. She enjoyed pranks and banter with male company, but she never once allowed a man to touch her in an intimate way. When anyone tried, Oshima reared like a wild horse and either attacked the offender, scratching his hands and face, or put him to shame by exposing him to public laughter, laughter she took great delight in.

Oshima vividly remembered how, at the age of six, she had been adopted into her foster family. Her natural mother had formed an obsessive hatred for Oshima, her youngest daughter. One evening, Oshima's father took her hand and led her out of the house to escape her mother's rage and a savage beating. Father and daughter wandered aimlessly through the countryside. It must have been toward the end of autumn, for red persimmons hung heavily from the branches of trees clustered around cheap food and tea stalls in the impoverished districts through which they passed. Her father often stopped at such places to allow his child to rest. He smoked and drank tea while Oshima munched on rice crackers and persimmons peeled and brought to her by the serving girl. With timid eyes, she looked around at her unfamiliar surroundings. The flaming red sunset was being swallowed by darkness, and a cold wind blew off the empty fields. Evening mist had begun to obscure isolated stands of trees and the houses in their shadows. Sheaves of rice hung out as offerings to the gods appeared dimly yellow against the dark earth. On the road in front of the stall, a workhorse, exhausted from the long day's labor, trudged wearily by. Why she did not know, but Oshima was moved to tears at the sight of the bleary eyes of the poor beast, docilely pulling its heavy wagon. Her father, at a loss for what to do with his daughter, also looked miserable.

She remembered being led to the shore of a wide expanse of water. Perhaps they had come to the ferry crossing at Ogu on the Sumida river. Faint light from the pearl-colored sky glinted on the surface of the slow-flowing dark water, and skiffs cast lonely shadows as they glided silently by. Waves lapped the bank of the river, and the monstrous shadow of a giant tree looming above Oshima swayed over the water. As she gazed at the quiet scene, her child's being was overcome by sensations of both dread and peace, and in silence she clung intently to her father's thin hand.

2

LATER, ON CONSIDERING what her stern, moralistic father might have intended that evening, Oshima could think of no reason why he had brought her to the edge of the river. Perhaps he wanted to take her across and leave her with a friend living on the other side.

That evening, however, her child's intuition had sensed something terrible, a cruel resolve, in the depths of her father's heart as he stood staring at the water. She was frightened. His eyes spoke of agonized indecision and regret.

Soon after she was born, Oshima had been sent away to be raised by relatives, and, by the time she was taken back in by her parents, she had become estranged from her strong-willed mother. On one occasion, irritated by Oshima's constant whimpering, her mother had pressed a pair of red-hot tongs against the child's tiny hand. With tears in her eyes, Oshima stared at the metal burning her flesh, but she obstinately refused to pull her hand away. This further aroused her mother's hatred.

"Stubborn little monster!" Mother's rage mounted, and she cursed her daughter.

As hereditary heads of the village, Oshima's family had been charged by the shogunate with collecting district taxes, and, during her childhood, her house was still much respected in the vicinity of Ōji. Her grandfather had once offered his enormous garden as a resting station for the pleasure excursions of members of the Tokugawa house, an honor that gave luster to her family's name and social standing in the area. That garden still exists as a public park for the local citizenry. As the heir to a long-established house of gardeners, gardening being an honorable profession that entitled him to enter the homes of the wealthy and wellborn, her father had made one mistake that damaged the reputation of his house; he had taken Oshima's mother, who was of low birth, as his second wife. She had been one of the serving girls in the cheap local restaurant where he would occasionally go to drink. After the marriage, the mother earned a reputation as a hard worker, but no one spoke well of her deportment or moral character.

Oshima was introduced to her foster family through an acquaintance of her father's who happened to pass by the ferry crossing at Ogu the evening Oshima and her father were there. Oshima's new parents, Mizushima and his wife, Otora, had barely been eking out a living from a paper mill, but, at about the time they adopted Oshima, they were blessed with a miraculous windfall. Their wealth increased dramatically, and they began buying local properties one after another. Oshima learned of the wondrous happening from snatches of conversations she overheard. It seemed to her like something out of a fairy tale. One winter evening, a wandering Buddhist monk, bearing an altar on his back and exhausted from his long pilgrimage, arrived at Mizushima's door and begged for a night's lodging. At dawn, as the monk departed, he foretold that unexpected good fortune would bless his host's house. A few days later, in the wake of the monk's visit, a huge sum of gold coins was found in a pile of harvested mulberry stalks. To search for the wandering monk and also to give thanks to various Shinto gods and Buddhist deities for their blessing, Mizushima later set off on a pilgrimage of his own, but he encountered no one resembling the monk. Be that as it may, from that time on only prosperity visited Oshima's foster family. Her new mother and father began lending sums of money to people in the town, and the couple watched in delight as their wealth increased.

"I wonder who on earth that monk was, the one who brought us such good fortune years ago?" Mizushima would exclaim after contributing generously to mendicant monks, who came on rare occasions to his gate. Then he would recount for Oshima his memories of the miraculous event. But Oshima had heard the story before.

She was more interested in her real parents and brothers and sisters. She had few occasions to visit them since she had come to live with her foster family.

3

As TIME PASSED, however, another version of the story took shape in Oshima's mind. According to information that she picked up at random from the talk of schoolmates who knew of her foster family's past, Oshima learned that, on that night so many years before, the wandering monk had suddenly taken ill and died at Mizushima's house. Tucked under his clothing, tied by a cord around his neck, was a purse heavy with gold coins. It was general knowledge that Oshima's foster parents had taken the money and kept it as their own. Oshima found this account more convincing, and it left her with an unpleasant feeling.

"Let them say what they please. When someone makes a little money, people will talk," her foster mother, Otora, replied with a forced smile after Oshima discreetly questioned her. But Oshima felt that the trust she had placed in her foster parents was being betrayed.

She even sensed that her hopes for happiness were doomed by fate. She did her best to avoid touching on the Mizushimas' secret and to be considerate and protective of their feelings, but she also experienced a new estrangement in her dealings with them.

On her way to the lavatory at night, Oshima had to pass through the lonely room containing the family Buddhist altar, the room where the monk was said to have stayed. It was the largest room in the house, its floor covered with warped old mats, and light did not penetrate into the interior even during the day. When Oshima got older, a storage area off the kitchen was turned into her sleeping quarters. Her foster parents' bedroom was next to the room in which the monk died. Passing through the large room at night, Oshima thought she saw the outstretched body of the pale monk still clutching at his purse, and her heart raced with fear. Was it not, she wondered, the vengeful spirit of the dead monk haunting the dreams of her foster father, causing him to call out and groan in his sleep after he went to bed early every evening? His moans awakened Oshima at night.

Even during the warm days of early spring, the interior of the house was damp and depressing. After a day spent sewing in the room fronting on the garden, Oshima's tired mind was infected by the gloom of the place. Brushing off the bits of thread clinging to her clothing, she hurried out to the paper mill, which stood in a clearing at the back of the house.

Sunlight streamed through the reed screen, warming the water that brimmed in the wooden trough for soaking mulberry bark. Cherry trees around the mill were on the verge of blooming. Paper was drying on numerous flat board racks set up in the clearing. In recent years, competition from a large paper factory established in Ōji had caused Mizushima to announce that he was going to quit the business, and he no longer put much effort into the mill. Most of the workmen had been laid off. A mulberry field near the main house had been turned into an elegant garden, with fashionably primitive wicket and fence and gate and attractive rocks and plantings. During the last few years, Mizushima had made numerous improvements on the residence. Not only that, Oshima heard he had recently purchased several other houses that had been mortgaged and foreclosed, though her foster parents did not tell her precisely where these were.

"Looks like work for the dirt poor!" Oshima remarked to Sakutarō. This young man was Mizushima's nephew, and she had been raised with him from an early age. He was smoking a cigarette as he crouched to tend the fires for boiling mulberry bark in cauldrons.

In the early spring sunlight, his pasty face with its wispy beard seemed all the more sickly.

"Haven't seen you make paper for a while," Oshima said.

"The old man's lost interest in it these days," Sakutarō replied, without looking up. "There isn't much chance of finding a purse of gold coins in this pile of mulberry."

"You're right about that!" Oshima laughed derisively.

4

As a child, Oshima was often taken to and from school by Sakutarō. For years, he had been sent out to work as a hand in the paper factory alongside women laborers, and he was also made to slave away at fieldwork and other arduous tasks during silkworm season. Nevertheless, the strong-willed Otora frequently scolded Sakutarō, and Oshima loathed him as if he were a pig. Exhausted from the endless hard work, Sakutarō would sometimes sleep late in the morning with the excuse that he was not feeling well. Otora would not permit it.

"The lazy bastard's still in bed while we're so busy! Think of the sort of people you come from!"

As she peered into the dirty closet where Sakutarō had crawled to sleep, Otora repeated the insults she always reproached him with. Her shrill voice reverberated in his mind. He was born to Mizushima's elder brother, a criminal, and a woman who was a wandering performer and prostitute. No one knew where she came from. Sakutarō's natural father had squandered his own inheritance on gambling and women and had become a burden on his younger brother. Then one day, relying on a relative, he left for Gunma prefecture on the chance of earning some money. There he was seduced by Sakutarō's mother. His circumstances were soon reduced to those of a beggar, and the two of them came straggling home. The woman, pregnant with Sakutarō when she arrived, gave birth but shortly thereafter abandoned the baby at Mizushima's and set off alone on a journey to an unknown destination. It was not until two or three years later that news came from Kisarazu, a place famous as a nest for criminal elements, that the child's natural father had died of illness.

Oshima often heard Otora admonish Sakutarō with the circumstances of his birth. How Otora loved repeating to Sakutarō the vivid description of his parents dragging their feet back home, both of them exhausted, with no money for train fare, their emaciated faces burned black and hard by the hot sun of summer and the harsh winds off the wild fields. When Sakutarō behaved in a way that was even a little lazy or sly, Otora would once again bring up the story of his parents' homecoming.

"If you'd stayed with that gang, mark my word, you'd be a beggar today! Go ahead, long for your real mother. Go to her, and see where it gets you!"

There were times when tears would run down Sakutarō's cheeks as he listened to Otora's story about his parents, but in the end he would simply laugh his obsequious laugh.

He was not really a homely person. Rather, his skin color and tone were poor and his eyes dull and dry, even from early adolescence. His stunted physical condition was the result of bad diet and being worked constantly at hard labor during the crucial period of his body's development. Ordered by his foster father to go out in rainy weather to bring Oshima home from school or sent in the evening to find Oshima, who in playing with her friends had drifted some distance away, Saku would have to track her down and carry the tired girl home in his arms or on his back. Saku now had occasion to stare in wonder at this same Oshima, with her thick, lustrous hair and ample flesh, growing so attractive that he scarcely recognized the girl he had known. The sight of Oshima working with the sleeves of her kimono tied up—her black hair done in the style of a young woman, the sensual swelling of her upper arms and chest glimpsed through the openings in her kimono beneath her arms—was enough to make him forget his feelings of envy toward her, feelings that had rankled for some time. On every occasion she could find, Otora made a point of reminding Saku that Oshima was born of far better family than he and that she was going to inherit Mizushima's wealth. Until recently, Oshima had been placed so far above him that he had wanted to curse her and everything she stood for.

5

AT ABOUT THIS TIME, Oshima came to regard Saku with utter contempt.

Late on a humid summer night, with all the sliding doors and windows to her room open, Oshima was drifting in and out of sleep in her mosquito netting. Her limbs felt dull and heavy, and the whining of the mosquitoes irritated her. She was suddenly shocked by Saku's pale face staring in at her from outside the netting.

"You fool! I'm going to tell mother!" she screamed.

Saku slunk away. For the first time, Oshima understood the significance of Saku's strange behavior and was struck by a fierce sense of having been insulted. Once she had wondered why he hovered so close to her as she worked in the fields, and there was the time she had discovered him peeping in as she bathed.

From then on, the mere sight of Saku offended her. So, when Oshima became vaguely aware that Mizushima intended to choose the hardworking Saku as her husband, the mere thought was enough to make her cringe in disgust. As his preference for Saku became apparent, Oshima began to yearn for her natural parents.

"Saku's my blood relation. If someone's going to inherit, it's only right it be him."

Mizushima and Otora appeared to be discussing the issue from time to time, and, when Oshima overheard her foster father's opinion, her heart grew heavy. The selfish impulse to resist welled up within her.

Saku viewed Oshima in a more familiar way. He tried to approach her with as little reserve as possible. When they were in the fields harvesting mulberry together, Saku would gravitate to where Oshima was laboring, no matter how busy he was. He began to show real interest in his work and was more obedient and deferential to his foster parents. This made him only more repugnant to Oshima.

Otora seemed to be secretly supporting another young man as Oshima's prospective husband and was spending a great deal of time with the elder brother of the candidate. The elder brother's name was Aoyagi, and, as a doctor with a general practice, he was well-known and popular in the area. The younger brother, whom Oshima knew slightly, was said to have graduated from a private college.

Oshima frequently saw Otora, who seemed accomplished at serving men, guide Aoyagi into the recesses of the house to heat and serve him sake while her husband was away. It was said that the average papermaker could process about forty bundles of mulberry stalks a day, but Otora was such a hard worker she could process eighty. She would ignore her good-natured husband and, with merciless vigilance, supervise the house's employees or lend money and collect debts. Yet, whenever the capable Otora met Aoyagi, she seemed flustered.

Oshima also found Aoyagi to be an agreeable person. He called her "the Kid" with apparent affection. Aoyagi had borrowed a considerable sum from Otora's husband for the construction of his new house.

6

LONG BEFORE SHE LEARNED of her proposed marriage to Saku, Oshima often went with Otora and Aoyagi to visit Nishi-Arai Daishi, a temple dedicated to the deified Buddhist saint Kūkai, and the nearby shrine of the Fox Deity. Oshima did not remember when her visits to the doctor Aoyagi began, but she saw him regularly for the treatment of congenital eye problems, and she soon became a friend of Ohana's, Aoyagi's niece, who lived with him.

Otora decided it was time for Oshima to have a new kimono, and she called the cloth merchant to Aoyagi's house and proposed that a kimono of the same design be made for Ohana as well. An appropriate fabric and pattern were chosen, the cloth was tailored into a set of kimonos, and, when Oshima and Ohana went out together in their new clothes, the neighbors assumed they were identical twins. At first, Otora and Aoyagi took only Oshima to the temple, but a few times they invited Ohana along as well. When Ohana did not come on these trips, the adults found a pretext to have Oshima visit the temple alone.

"We'll stop here for a rest," Otora declared, in front of a restaurant. "You're the one with the bad eyes, so you go ahead and pray to the gods. Take your time. Uncle Aoyagi has come along for entertainment, and he won't have fun without a drink. And you know how seldom I get away from the house."

Once the party had settled in a room in a separate building connected to the main restaurant by a bridge, Otora produced a few coins and placed them in Oshima's purse. She then sent Oshima on her way. The restaurant was about two and a half miles from the temple.

The early summer sun was hot, and sweat was soon running down the plump Oshima's back. Her makeup became spotted with perspiration, and she often stopped to take out her mirror and repowder her face. In the garden of the restaurant at the foot of the hill, azaleas bloomed in wild profusion, and brightly colored carp swam lazily in the pond, just like in a painting. She would have enjoyed staying there with the adults: after all, she had been working as hard as anyone and deserved a rest, too. But she felt uncomfortable in the room with Aoyagi and her foster mother, who were obviously ill at ease in her presence. Oshima had been brought up to humor her foster mother, and, if she had learned one thing, it was to be sensitive to Otora's whims. To please both of them, she readily agreed to go on by herself. She hurried out of the restaurant and set off for the temple.

In the immediate neighborhood, there were similar restaurants and four or five tea stalls, but she soon passed by them and found herself on a road that ran through rice paddies. Fields and forests seemed green and alive, and the sky was beautifully clear. On the curving, dusty road, she glimpsed clusters of fellow pilgrims on their way to the temple. In the shade of the forest to her left, filthy lepers prostrated themselves in supplication, striking their heads on the ground. One of them appeared ready to rush out and follow her to beg for alms. Oshima quickly opened her coin purse, threw some coins at the beggar, and hurried past him.

7

FOLLOWING THE SHADOWS of others on the twisting road, Oshima came to the straight main thoroughfare leading to the temple. She was swept along in the crowd of people, carts, and rickshas. Among the groups of men and women who seemed to come from backwater neighborhoods in Asakusa or Honjo, Oshima spied the occasional well-dressed, respectable young lady or fashionable young wife. There were also young dandies with gold-rimmed glasses and hand-rolled cigarettes tucked behind their ears. Moved by a gentle sympathy at the sight of so much humanity around her, the lone Oshima walked briskly through the dust raised by straw sandals and wooden geta. As she strode on, her underskirt felt pleasant against her hot, plump legs. She had ceased thinking about Otora and Aoyagi.

Various shops and stalls lined the avenue leading up to the temple. Some sold good-luck ornaments such as papier-mâché tigers and Daruma tumbling dolls; others sold rice-millet cakes and chopped toffee. She noticed shellfish being grilled for sale: *sazae* cooking in their own shells or clams baking over coals. Festive music blared from behind the main gate of the temple. Oshima rambled among the stalls set up at random inside the temple grounds. Fried dough, sugar cookies, and white-rice jelly, sweets that she had not seen for several years, caught her attention. She headed up the steps to the central hall of the temple. The old-fashioned, countrified atmosphere of the place depressed her, but she purchased a number of protective amulets and talismans to please her foster mother.

On leaving the main hall, Oshima roamed around the expansive temple compound, halting to observe some sort of sea mammal on exhibit and a rural, itinerant juggler. She looked for but could not find the beautiful young women who arrived at the temple with her. To pass the time, she loitered for a while in a rough, barren playground where cherry trees had recently been planted. Then she went around back to the cemetery. She witnessed an old peasant receiving the incantation of sacred waters from a priest, and she paused in front of rows of statues of Saint Kūkai, a candle burning in front of each figure. In a nearby grove, a crowd had formed to see a scrawny monkey in a sailor's suit walking a tightrope. Oshima watched for a time but soon grew bored and left.

She bought a bottle of lemon soda at a tea stall and sat outside to drink it and rest. By the time she set off to rejoin her foster mother, it was quite late in the day. A cool wind blew off the rice paddies, and, in the distance, factory smoke from the Senju industrial district formed a heavy, elongated cloud over the fields. Tired, Oshima felt a confused sense of disappointment.

Back at the restaurant, Oshima found Aoyagi in the middle of the cluttered room sleeping off the sake he had drunk. Otora's face was flushed as well, and she was picking her teeth with a toothpick.

"You're probably so hungry you can scarcely walk," Otora observed cheerfully. "Did you receive the incantation of the sacred waters and drink the water like I told you?"

"Yes, I drank a lot." Oshima lied without compunction.

Otora ordered dinner for Oshima, waited until she had finished, and then collected her coat and helped Aoyagi on with his and prepared to leave. By the time they had returned to their own neighborhood, the sun had set, and lamps had been lit in the surrounding houses. Frogs were croaking in the quiet fields.

"Thanks for giving us the day off," Otora declared loudly at the entrance of her house, but there was no response. Her husband was absorbed in some task in the back.

8

OSHIMA BECAME NERVOUS at Mizushima's silence, as if his resentment were directed against her. He refused at first to come in for dinner, and, when he did, he ate in silence and returned immediately to his account books. "I'll massage your shoulders?" she offered, as she saw him put down his brush. She circled to his back, trying to take the place of her foster mother in regaining his good humor. Since the age of nine or ten, Oshima had been in the habit of massaging her foster father.

After a brief rest, Otora put away the good clothing worn for the day's outing and then locked all the entrances. As she brusquely straightened up the mess made in her absence, she began gossiping with her husband about the restaurant she had visited that day. Mizushima had frequented the establishment years before.

Otora was the daughter of a farming family living eight or nine miles away, a family that also operated a small-scale paper mill. Her natural mother was a Tokyo native whom her father had had an affair with as a young man in Tokyo. Otora was well acquainted with people and places in the city. Mizushima used the restaurant to conduct business; he had met Otora there, and they had become friends. Oshima had heard this before from Otora. In those days, Mizushima was barely able to maintain his household, and Otora, who was raised by a stepmother, tended to become despondent, but, when the two married, they joined together as one and worked their hearts out.

Otora often spoke to Oshima of the hardships she had experienced in those early days, yet, as she and her husband had prospered during the past two or three years, Otora's resolve had begun to waver. Little by little, she felt herself growing distant from her husband, who knew nothing of the pleasures of the world. Perhaps it was in reaction to those years of self-denial that she now was being tempted by a life of promiscuity.

After massaging her foster parents, Oshima was at last allowed to go to bed. She soon fell into a sound sleep as she recalled the exciting scenes acted out between Otora and Aoyagi that day. The croaking of frogs echoed drowsily in her ears, and her strong, youthful limbs felt heavy and hot.

The next morning, Oshima's foster parents went about their work as if nothing had happened.

When their excursions included Aoyagi's niece, Ohana, Otora and Aoyagi stayed at the same restaurant, and Oshima and Ohana were sent to amuse themselves in the Asakusa district. Oshima and Ohana hired a ricksha at Ueno station and proceeded to Asakusa. They visited the famous Goddess of Mercy at the Sensōji temple, then paid for admission to the nearby amusement park, "The Flower Palace." The two young women walked hand in hand through the crowds, but Oshima continued to imagine what was going on at the restaurant.

Otora also called on Aoyagi's wife and invited her on a day trip to Tokyo. The young woman, who appeared shy and retiring, innocently accompanied her. On their return, Otora dropped in at Aoyagi's house and played the part of the elder sister counseling the younger. The wife did not reveal that she felt insulted. She dealt with Otora in a calm and polite manner.

9

WAS IT THE SUMMER of that next year? It was on a day when the two frames of silkworms entrusted to Oshima's care were in the pupa stage. Otora concluded a long argument with her husband by changing her clothes and storming out of the house.

Hurt by her husband's objections to the various sums of money that she had lent Aoyagi, Otora counterattacked with ferocious insults. Mizushima had a low, meek voice, and, as Otora became ever more forceful in her arguments, he was silenced. He tried to mollify his wife but could not resist resuming his complaints.

"If you'll recall, your life hasn't been one of great rectitude. When people learn how you got your start, you'll be ashamed to show your face in public."

Oshima, tending the silkworms with mulberry leaves, heard Otora's shrill accusation, and she was frozen in fear for a moment. She immediately remembered the dead monk. Her foster father's pitiful sputtering faded into silence.

She did not know the actual amount lent to Aoyagi, but, starting with the money that he had borrowed to build his house, and including the cash Otora frequently took to him, it was probably a considerable sum. Oshima could see with her own eyes that Aoyagi was living far more extravagantly the past year or so. She knew her foster mother supplied Aoyagi with small sums of money and goods, all of which she kept secret from her husband.

She had gone out with Otora and Aoyagi one last time in the winter, but even Otora had begun to hesitate to take the nearly sixteen-year-old Oshima with her. By the spring, Otora and Aoyagi had changed their meeting place and no longer patronized the restaurant.

Mizushima had started the quarrel about noon with questions concerning some money not accounted for. The argument expanded to a subject that he had not touched on for some time, the uncollected loan to Aoyagi. In his deliberate, tedious way, he demanded explanations for her odd behavior in a number of situations that he had witnessed in recent months.

Otora had the final word when she declared that they should divide the property exactly in half and separate. She left, and Oshima next heard her opening and shutting the drawers of her wardrobe chests, though, when she departed, she took no clothing or other possessions with her.

"Please, Mother! Calm down, and don't leave! What will happen to me if you go?" Oshima tearfully pleaded, but Otora did not even turn to glance at her adopted daughter.

That evening, Mizushima sent Oshima out to search for his wife. Oshima wandered around the neighborhood and checked at Aoyagi's but could not find her.

One day, while her foster mother was still away and Oshima was busy with the silkworms, Oshima happened to see her foster father airing an enormous quantity of yen bills in the large room fronting on the garden. The last time he had done this, Otora was visiting relatives in the city. Bundles of paper currency were laid out to air in the sunny areas of the large room.

10

OSHIMA KNEW THAT Mizushima had sent postcards to several households he was acquainted with, but the only reply was from Otora's family, and that arrived after Otora had returned.

For some reason, Oshima's foster father came into the silkworm room where Oshima was working and stood beside her staring down at the insects, which had just entered the cocoon-weaving phase. Some had become hard and translucently blue and were already spitting out their fine thread.

"I suppose your mother has warned you not to talk to me about certain things," Mizushima suddenly blurted out. It was not the first time that he had questioned Oshima in his wife's absence.

"What? No, nothing," Oshima replied, blushing.

Her foster father did not question her further, but Oshima felt she understood his weakness in dealing with Otora.

Otora returned that evening with an attitude that she had spent too much time visiting relatives and was glad to be back in her own home. Seated near the entrance, her husband was going over his accounts, but Otora said nothing to him and instead addressed Oshima with the brief greeting that she was home. Otora went to the family room off the kitchen, sat down, both legs outstretched, and gazed with satisfaction at her garden. The deep green of the foliage was as fresh and vivid as an oil painting.

Oshima picked up the kimono and sweaty underskirts her foster mother had thrown off and hung them on the bamboo drying racks in the room with a pleasant breeze. Then she went to make tea.

"It was a good chance to catch up with old friends and relatives," Otora told Oshima. Otora had descended to the garden to bathe, and Oshima was rinsing off her naked foster mother's back with rainwater from a barrel. She had visited the family that her younger half sister had married into and the house of a married childhood friend. All lived in the crowded downtown area of Tokyo. Not one had established a secure, comfortable life. After a day or two of living with such people, Otora would grow disgusted and move on. As Otora and her husband had grown more prosperous, they had distanced themselves from their former friends. They also had fewer and fewer contacts with Otora's relatives.

Her bath done, Otora showed her husband the numerous gifts— salted rice crackers, seaweed, and the like—that she had brought from Tokyo. Bothered by insects after dinner, she withdrew to the safety of the mosquito netting in her room.

Oshima had difficulty sleeping nights, so she often took a bench outside and sat there to cool herself as the evening mist was absorbed by the earth. At times, young women and men from the town gathered around her. Gossip about love affairs entertained all present, and the young men sometimes angered the young women with their mischief.

Saku, as always the last to bathe, came out fastening his cotton robe and timidly approached Oshima.

"Here comes the fool again!" Oshima declared abruptly and went back inside.

11

THE PROSPECT OF OSHIMA's marriage to Aoyagi's brother dissolved because of Mizushima's opposition. The relationship between Otora and Aoyagi was breaking up at about the same time. Otora sensed that Oshima and others had hinted of her affair to her husband, and the thought of being found out was disagreeable to her. It had also become obvious that Aoyagi and his wife were conspiring in their greed to wring as much money out of Otora as they could.

From the winter to the spring of Oshima's sixteenth year, her foster parents tried to convince her to marry Saku. He was to inherit, and Oshima would ultimately control the family property. Oshima refused, and, because this offended her foster parents' sense of propriety, she briefly returned to her natural parents. All the while she was sewing her trousseau, she was not certain whom she would marry. Yet, from time to time, she thought vaguely of Aoyagi's brother. He had studied mechanics at a school in Tokyo. Since he had found a position in Fukagawa, she had occasionally seen him going to work early in the morning dressed in a Western-style suit and hat. She had never spoken to him and did not know what he thought of her. Meeting on the street, they had bowed to one another, but he had made little impression on Oshima. When Aoyagi and Otora brought up the possibility of marriage to the younger brother, she avoided discussing it.

A letter in a beautiful envelope was delivered to Oshima by the dim-witted Ohana. Neither Oshima nor Ohana could read the small characters written with a fountain pen on Western-style stationery, but Oshima could at least discern that Aoyagi's brother was dissatisfied with both his own family and Oshima's. She faintly sensed his sympathy for her unhappiness at being subservient to her family's wishes, though she was also embarrassed by his concern. She later crumpled up the letter and threw it away. When, with some pride, Oshima spoke to Otora about the letter, her foster mother's response was laughter.

"He's a strange fellow," Otora declared. "He says he doesn't want to be adopted into another family, but then he sends you a letter!"

Once convinced her foster parents had decided that Saku would be her husband, Oshima was so disappointed she stopped working. Sensing Oshima's unhappiness, Otora repeated the old story of when the six-year-old Oshima was first brought to her foster family.

"They say your father didn't know what to do with you and was going to throw you in the river. If you'd stayed with your real mother, she'd have tortured you, and you'd be a crippled freak today." Otora stressed the cruelty of Oshima's natural parents.

12

No one in the neighborhood had been informed about Oshima's coming marriage to Saku, so, when Oshima heard of it from a customer who lived some distance away, she was shocked. How pitiful she must seem. She detested Saku, who was apparently bragging about his coming marriage to her.

He had not changed in the least from the Saku who once took her home from school, the Saku she scolded and forced to wait outside because she was not ready. The mere touch of his hand on her sandal made her shiver with displeasure.

Saku had learned nothing from experience, and the talk of marriage emboldened him to approach Oshima. While she was putting on her makeup, he drew near to her and stared with a silly grin on his face.

"Stay away from me!" Oshima screamed, pushing him away.

"You shouldn't be so mean," Saku said, as he trudged out of the room.

She wedged a stick against the sliding door of her room to prevent Saku from entering.

"I hate him, I hate him. I'd rather die than marry Saku!" Oshima told Otora in Saku's presence, and she stubbornly refused even to consider the match.

"I hear Saku's been chosen as the lucky groom!" Oshima was teased with similar remarks at several of the houses where she went to collect accounts.

She seemed able to walk forever, and she was quick and articulate, so, in her mid-teens, Oshima was assigned to make the rounds of the family's customers and debtors. Her energetic and amusing style of doing business was popular with all the family's customers. As she grew accustomed to the work, she became even more popular. Her cautious foster father was not altogether happy at this development, and he occasionally scolded her.

"What's the difference! I'm not costing you any money!" the annoyed Oshima replied. "You'll never expand your business if you're stingy."

Although he worried about the generous way in which Oshima did business, the meek Mizushima also found her useful.

"That's a lie," Oshima declared, denying that she was engaged to be married to Saku.

"But I heard it from Saku himself," said one customer, studying Oshima.

"You think you can believe that idiot?" Oshima replied, with a scornful laugh. By the time she fled to the home of her natural parents, Oshima was encountering such rumors wherever she went.

"Then what kind of man do you want to marry?" Otora finally asked.

"I don't want a sluggard like Saku. I'd like a husband who hopes to accomplish something in the world, a man who wants to live with a little style. I don't want to spend my life making paper or calculating interest on small loans."

13

THE TRADITIONAL HOLIDAYS of New Year and the Festival of Souls, Obon, in the summer, were about the only chances that Oshima had to spend the night with her natural family, so it did not surprise Oshima when Otora came to fetch her after she had been gone only a few days.

As a child, Oshima, accompanied by Saku, visited her natural family bearing gifts of bags of sugar or salted salmon. But, since she had taken over collecting accounts, which gave her access to the keys of the drawers and cabinets containing money, she was able to bring her family geta, items of clothing, and other more expensive presents. Oshima normally did not get along with her older sister, and her younger sister, influenced by her mother, regarded Oshima with a certain contempt. Oshima enjoyed forcing her sisters to bow in gratitude for the fine gifts she brought them. Her pride in giving was not limited to her immediate blood relations: Oshima took pleasure in making gifts of money or goods to a number of people associated with her foster parents' business. Mizushima sternly closed his pocketbook to the most pitiable pleas from poor farm laborers, but, when Oshima intervened, he could not maintain his habitual stinginess. Workmen, followed by pimps collecting payments to brothels—even such debtors as these were at times recipients of Oshima's generosity. On meeting Oshima in the street, they would bow with a sincere sense of gratitude and respect.

Oshima's natural father attempted to hand over the outside gardening work to his eldest son, but the son's addiction to women and drink caused him to disappoint his father's expectations, so Father was forced to resume his trade. He was so busy that Oshima seldom saw him. At mealtimes, Oshima's natural mother made Oshima wretched with poisonous insults.

When her mother saw Oshima working hard, pulling weeds in the large garden and watering an ancient tree that her father did not want to lose, she yelled out of the window: "Go on, work your heart out from dawn to dark, you'll never inherit a thing from us!" In the huge garden enclosed by a large formal gate and fence, there were a number of different-sized pots containing old pines and plum trees. Just outside the garden was an area planted with dozens of pines. Another field contained a variety of small shrubs and trees for gardens. Oshima had heard that her father had recently divided up these scattered properties among her siblings. Even the land on which he had constructed his flimsy little house for his retirement was deeded over to one of his children.

"What would I do with a tiny bit of land and a few trees? I don't desire the little you have," Oshima replied as she came over barefoot to refill her watering can from the well in the kitchen. "I'm not lusting after Mizushima's money either!"

"Aren't you generous! Pride has twisted your nature. That's why people hate you."

"The only person who hates me is you, mother. I don't know anyone else who hates me."

"I'm right about you! I'd hoped that by seeing how other decent people live, you might be improved a little, but you just get worse and worse."

"I really don't need your motherly concern. After all, it's not like you've ever treated me like your daughter." Oshima turned away and bustled into the kitchen.

14

OSHIMA WAS ALMOST FINISHED with the chores, but, tired of quarreling with her mother, she went out again with her large watering can to water the potted plants. Her eyes clouded with tears as she brushed factory soot off a pine tree.

"Thanks for the help," the young people called to her as they came home from work.

"I have to keep busy," Oshima called back. She pushed back a strand of hair that fell in bold relief against her white cheek. Her cheerful voice came from behind the green foliage. But Oshima was remembering the pain of the beatings she had received from her mother as a child. The scar inflicted by the burning tongs that her mother had pressed against her flesh when she was four still marked the palm of her hand. Saying that Oshima told tales to her father, her mother pinched and twisted her lips; or, claiming that Oshima was teasing her younger sister, her mother pushed her head so deeply into the snow piled under the eaves that Oshima thought she might suffocate. When her mother served meals to her sons, she insisted that the hungry Oshima's staring at the food was greedy impudence, and she gave her daughter nothing. Her mother would lock her in a shed containing hoes, pruning shears, and shovels and leave her there sobbing until dark. Oshima would stamp and scream in rage.

Oshima's father pitied his daughter and released her, all the while attempting to calm his wife.

"I've had so many children, and none has been as stubborn and defiant as her," the mother argued, in a tone that suggested she wished to grind the life out of her daughter.

Oshima wondered whether her mother was like the goddess Hariti, who cared only for her own children and ate the children of others. With the exception of Oshima, her mother loved her other offspring equally.

At dusk, Oshima put her tools away in the storage shed and went in for dinner. Sitting by the brazier, her father, with a dour expression on his face, had begun drinking the measured amount of wine that he indulged in every evening. Outside, the colors of night were spreading slowly, and Oshima heard the lowing of cattle from a nearby pasture. The children playing detective on the road had gone home. The light of the stars had softened, suggesting the coming of spring.

"Let Oshima stay for a month or two. When we find her a place to go into domestic service, she'll be able to take care of herself," her father said, in an attempt to mollify his wife, who was complaining about her daughter's presence. Pricking up her ears, but not listening too obviously, Oshima was taking her eating utensils to the kitchen.

"Wait and see! I'll accomplish something that'll make your eyes pop out!" Controlling the rage welling up within her against her mother, Oshima left the room with as much dignity as possible. She thought she might like to try her hand at the business that the old man Nishida was involved in. Nishida, the intermediary in Oshima's adoption, had recently started supplying feed for the horses of the

Japanese army. Oshima bitterly resented her mother's pronounce-
ments that her older sister was blissfully happy with her new husband, a steady, hardworking employee of the family. Nonetheless, to
escape the proposed marriage to Saku, she was determined never to
cross the threshold of Mizushima's house again. As she ate dinner,
Oshima became dizzy with anger.

15

ON THE AFTERNOON OTORA came to take Oshima home,
Oshima's father happened to be in the vicinity of the house. At a site
two or three blocks away, he was teaching several young men how to
prepare the roots of a large Japanese red pine so the tree could be
transported to a customer's garden.

Oshima guided Otora to the guest room and left to call her
father, as her mother had instructed. Since coming to live with her
cruel natural mother, Oshima had realized how much affection she
felt for Otora, who had raised her with such kindness for so many
years. She longed for her foster family and the familiar people and
environs associated with them.

"Oshima, don't you think it's wrong for you to go on being a burden here day after day? I've come to take you home," Otora declared
as she entered, and Oshima suddenly felt there was no point in resisting. She was moved almost to tears.

"'You haven't disciplined the girl. That's why she disobeys us.
She won't change now. Leave her where she is.' That's what my husband told me to do, but, when I think of how I've looked after her all
these years, hoping she'd be the one to care for me in my old age, I
have to give her another chance."

As she was making tea, Oshima heard these opening remarks
that Otora addressed to her natural mother, and, though her mother
loved to berate Oshima in the most ridiculous terms to anyone who
would listen, today, for some reason, she contented herself with a
simple, modest reply.

Oshima's father was not articulate in social situations, and he
looked troubled as he returned. He went around to the kitchen
entrance, washed his face and hands at the well, and came in. A day
or two earlier, Oshima had asked her father a number of questions

about the value and size of the property that he had recently prom-ised to leave her if he could keep the transaction secret from her mother. The amount of land was seven-eighths of an acre, and its conservative value, including trees, was probably not less than ten thousand yen. Oshima was reassured by her father's offer, but, at the same time, she had concluded that, as long as there was light in her mother's eyes, she would not take possession of her share.

"How much land does our family own altogether?" Oshima had then asked her father.

His general estimate of eight acres was about what Oshima had thought. These lands included the family's vegetable fields and rice paddies. However, because of his many children and his eldest son's dissipation, much of his land was mortgaged. The eldest son, Sōtarō, had left home the previous autumn to make money in the provinces, and his lover, a former prostitute, was still living with him there. Sōtarō's legal wife and their three-year-old child were taken in by the wife's parents, who were living in Tokyo. The only person resem-bling an adult male at home to help her father was Oshima's fifteen-year-old brother.

From what Oshima had seen over the past five days, she sensed that her natural family's situation was beginning to deteriorate. She also thought she understood the reasons for her mother's anxiety.

16

OSHIMA WANDERED THROUGH the field of pine trees after her father went in. If she stayed here, she and her mother would con-tinue to snarl at each other. The more they quarreled, the more rebellious she would become, and the more her hatred would grow. Her mother's treatment of her as a child, which she had managed to forget for a long time, would go on festering in her mind. The thought of her younger brothers and sisters each receiving ten or twenty thousand yen while she would not inherit a handful of dirt convinced Oshima that she could not depend on her natural family. But she also knew that, if she returned to the Mizushimas, they would pressure her to marry Saku. She had learned from numerous custom-ers and others associated with her foster family that the proposed marriage could not be dismissed as rumor but was as certain as words carved in stone. Saku disgusted her. The balding spots around the collar of his scrawny neck, his hair curling around his ears like a shaggy dog, his red eyes, his halting speech, the despicable character of a slave—the very familiarity born of having been raised with Saku made him seem all the more ugly and contemptible in Oshima's eyes. She could not conceive of spending her entire life with the man. She took it for granted that her natural mother would condemn her for refusing the match, but she thought it terribly cruel for her father to hint he would agree to Saku being forced on her.

When her parents finally called her, Oshima wiped away her tears and entered.

"I've been busy these days and haven't had time to ask about your situation, but what exactly do you think you're doing?" the father asked a defiant-looking Oshima.

Oshima sat in silence as her father picked up his pipe in his hard hands. Her eyes were moist.

"Consider the debt you owe your mother! Aren't you being selfish when you insist you hate Saku? Think about your conduct!" her father continued.

"I won't marry him!" Oshima replied, the muscles in her face twitching. "Anything else, I'll do anything else to repay my mother's kindness, but I won't marry him."

Her father, lighting his pipe, said nothing, but her natural mother glared with hatred at her daughter and declared, "Oshima, I won't permit you to speak like that to a guest! Have you no sense of common courtesy!"

"Why do you dislike Sakutarō so?" Otora asked, leaning over to fill and light her extravagant silver pipe. "In any case, we'll treat your feelings about him as a separate problem. Come home with me today. If you continue to feel the way you do, I won't force you. People in the neighborhood are gossiping about you. Let's return, and we can talk later," Otora continued, trying to placate Oshima, and she slowly put her pipe away.

It required a great deal more persuasion before Oshima nodded in agreement, but, when they did leave, Oshima felt no regret, for now she clearly understood her relationship with her natural family.

"Thank you for your hospitality. I'm sorry if I've inconvenienced you," Oshima said in farewell and followed Otora outside.

There was no change in the animated tone and familiarity of the conversation between the two women.

"You shouldn't despise a man just because he's ugly," Otora argued on the way back, but finally Oshima made Otora promise not to mention the name Saku again.

17

OTORA EXPLAINED HOW SHE had told people in the neighborhood that Oshima was away caring for her ill mother. Oshima was not to contradict this story.

"And don't be too mean to Sakutarō. I know he acts like a fool, but he isn't a bad person. As young as he is, he's never bought one woman, and now he's working so hard, all because he wants to marry you. If you set him to work and you took over the business side of things, you'd be an unbeatable team! I'm certain you'll come to see it my way," Otora lectured Oshima.

Oshima thought there was something strange in Otora's words. She vowed that she would not let herself be deceived.

Returning to her foster parents' house, Oshima discovered that Saku had been sent away on an errand. Mizushima, out back by the paper mill, came in as soon as he heard his wife's voice. Controlling her temper, Oshima bowed and apologized to her foster father as Otora had instructed. But, when Otora began speaking about Oshima's deep regret over what she had done and how she felt it was all her fault, Oshima's eyes darkened with anger. This house as well now seemed intolerable. She sensed that she had chosen a path leading inevitably to disaster.

"You can't have forgotten how your father in Ōji told your mother he'd drowned you in the Sumida river," Mizushima stated ominously, bringing up that old story again.

Oshima defiantly turned her head away, and tears streamed down her cheeks.

"People who forget where they come from will never amount to anything," her foster father preached, as the impatient Oshima made motions to rise and leave. "What'd they say at Ōji? They couldn't possibly believe you have right on your side."

With downcast eyes, Oshima sat in silence, but her nerves were electric, and she could not endure much more.

Otora recognized that the moment had come to end the interview, and she sent Oshima out to perform some chores, providing her the opportunity to escape at last from her foster father. As Oshima was cleaning her room—folding her clothing, putting away various objects, sweeping up the dust that had accumulated while she was away—she began to realize how thoroughly she was being intimidated.

That evening, Oshima went out to the fields to pick fragrant herbs for the morning's broth. Coming back inside, she caught sight of Saku, who had just returned and was sitting down to his evening meal. He glared spitefully at Oshima but said nothing. Later, as Oshima was preparing the meal trays for breakfast, Saku brought in his dirty bowl and dishes to be washed. As usual, he wore a silly grin.

"They're filthy! Put them over there," Oshima commanded, and she refused to touch them.

18

THE SECOND TIME Oshima ran away from her foster family was just after her wedding to Saku, toward the end of autumn of the same year.

In the lingering summer heat, Mizushima set off for a hot spring in Gunma prefecture to recuperate from an illness, but he returned earlier than expected, having used little more than half the money he had taken with him. He showed a new sense of urgency in his concern about Oshima's marriage. Shortly after his arrival home, the trousseau that Oshima had worked on in the spring was taken out and necessary items purchased for it.

During silkworm-raising season that summer, Oshima showed little interest in the tasks she had become so proficient at over the years. Her lack of enthusiasm for her work caused Mizushima to fret in his sickbed. Rather than nursing her foster father with food and medicine and washing his dirty clothing and bedding, Oshima idled away the hours in profitless visits to customers in the town and surrounding countryside. Tracing her memories back to childhood, Oshima was struck by the futility of all her efforts to gain the admiration of her foster parents. She despaired that her diligent labor, rough though it may have been, had done nothing for her economic or social position. At other times, though, she was delighted by the prospect of receiving new clothing for the wedding, or she felt a vague pride that, in the future, she would be an heiress to substantial property. Then she was overjoyed by her good fortune in being the only daughter of two people far more loving than her true parents.

The people around her all appeared to respect her. From Nishida, the old man supplying horse feed to the army, to the tenant farmers dependent on her foster family and the others whom she had helped so often, everyone seemed to be looking forward to the day when she would take control of her foster family's businesses.

"Don't worry! I'll take care of you. When you're ready to lose everything like I am, your little debt means nothing," Oshima told the obsequiously bowing man who was making excuses for not repaying a loan. She enjoyed the role of the generous female boss.

Even while her foster father was ill at home, Aoyagi began calling on Otora again. His visits increased after Mizushima departed for the hot spring. It was not just to avoid the couple that Oshima spent more and more time away from home. She had lost affection for the house that she had lived in securely for ten years and now had no desire to spend the rest of her life there. She would often enter the homes of friendly customers and spend half the day in idle gossip. Filling in for a local shopkeeper, she exchanged pleasantries with his regular customers or dressed the hair of his wife, with whom she got on well.

"I wonder if I should try to find a job in Tokyo for a few years." Oshima was moved by the strong impulse to find some sort of rewarding work.

"You're joking," the wife commented, laughing.

"No, I'm serious. I'm sick to death of that family."

"If you leave, it'll be a great loss for them."

"Probably not. They're the sort of people who'll never trust their affairs to me. 'What stunt will she pull next?' I think I terrify them!" Oshima declared, good-humoredly.

With a quick, practiced hand, Oshima undid the wife's chignon and combed her hair straight up. The woman's scalp hurt, as if she were being lifted up by her hair.

19

OSHIMA THOUGHT OF SEARCHING for a suitable occupation and began inquiring of people she knew. Going into the city, she wandered about to get an idea of what was available. She found no work appropriate to her skills, no vocation to which she could devote herself wholeheartedly. She had barely graduated from primary school, and clerical work was beyond her intellectual abilities.

She considered going to an employment broker, and she even walked back and forth outside the entrance to one's shop, but she was revolted by an ignorant-looking woman, who appeared to have just run away from the provinces, and the seedy umbrella, cloth bundles, and leather-covered geta of other job seekers. She was not able to work up the courage to descend to their level.

On her trips to the city, Oshima often did not return when evening approached; instead, she whiled away the hours by herself on the hill at Ueno. Below, lights from the lamps and lanterns of eating places, bars, and merchants' stalls merged with the yellowish green of the willows, and shadowy streetcars and crowds moved about as if in a dream. Oshima found herself thinking of a benefactor's son who had emigrated to America. It occurred to her that she might steal money for passage from Mizushima and go overseas, relying on her acquaintance to help her there.

When Oshima asked Nishida for his opinion of her plan to emigrate, the old man dismissed it without a second thought.

"What dimwit would row the boat this far, have the destination in sight, and then give up all that property by running away?"

According to the old man, her foster parents' fortune was far greater than Oshima imagined. Liquid assets and real estate included, her family was worth at least one hundred thousand yen. The amount of currency stored in the cash box under the floor was certainly not a trivial sum. There was probably truth to the rumor that Mizushima still retained some of the monk's gold coins in the box.

The old man, with his numerous young children, was one of the people who got his start by borrowing capital from Oshima's foster father. The amount he still owed was substantial. With irritating frequency, he repeated the platitude: If you aren't greedy, you'll be at a disadvantage your whole life.

Oshima had thus decided to return to her foster family. However, until a prospective husband other than Saku was decided on through the mediation of the old man or Aoyagi, she was prepared to leave her foster family at the mere suggestion that she marry Saku.

20

AFTER PLANS FOR THE WEDDING were announced, Aoyagi seemed to come every day, whenever he had a moment, to consult secretly with Oshima's foster parents. He brought decorations for the "Island of Everlasting Youth," a traditional standing wedding ornament, and a pair of scrolls, one the painting of a crane and the other of a tortoise, symbols of long life. Aoyagi hung these above the other decorations in the alcove and stared with admiration at his handiwork.

"This time for certain you won't run off, Oshima. My brother's a good-looking young man," he said, gazing at Oshima. She had not made the rounds of her customers for several days. Aoyagi's hair was thinning, and a few silver hairs glinted under the light, but his face was lustrous and his eyes full of life. The younger brother was not as handsome as the older. Still, Oshima was vastly relieved when she heard that, after all the turmoil, he had been chosen as her husband. He had moved to a boardinghouse close to the factory he was commuting to, and he no longer lived with his older brother. Oshima had not seen him since the New Year's celebration. His letter had strangely alienated her, but now imagining what he would look like on the night of the wedding filled her with both anticipation and self-doubt.

On the morning of the wedding, Oshima was very nervous. Digging up taro root in the dew-covered field was the only work she did that day. Autumn winds rustled through the dry stalks of harvested corn and millet, and formations of migrating birds called to each other as they flew away in the distant, cloudless sky.

Full realization that she would be given in marriage that evening came in the afternoon as she was having her hair done in formal ceremonial fashion, but, on considering that her groom was the younger brother of the familiar Aoyagi, who had been teasing and joking with her since she was twelve or thirteen, she found it difficult to maintain a mood of strict decorum. Even in Otora's presence, Aoyagi could not keep his eyes off Oshima. In her new clothing, she seemed to blossom into charming womanhood before him. The salacious remarks that he directed at Oshima warned Otora that she should not relax her vigilant watch on the man.

Given the whole day off, Sakutarō had been to the barber, returned and bathed, then dressed in his finest clothing. He grinned broadly at the sight of Oshima and stared in wonder at the lists and random stacks of wedding gifts. By the time the cook from a local restaurant arrived with a cart full of food, close friends of the family in formal dress were bustling back and forth helping with the preparations. The whole house seemed suddenly alive with activity. The old man Nishida hurried from one person to the next whispering conspiratorially.

"If you run away tonight, the rest of your life will be ruined. Be patient, and leave everything to me." There was an urgency in the old man's voice as he drew close to Oshima to hiss this warning. He found her in a daze, standing with her back against a chest of drawers.

21

THE HAIRDRESSER STAYED on to act as go-between at the wedding, and, as she was helping Oshima into the three black silk undercoats customarily worn by women during winter ceremonial occasions, Oshima's natural father from Ōji arrived wearing old-fashioned *haori* and *hakama*. Oshima's natural mother, who was not accustomed to appearing before large numbers of people, declared from the first that she would not attend her daughter's wedding.

Her father, who once considered drowning his daughter in the river, was not in the least concerned with whom Oshima married so long as she was in a position to inherit her foster family's property. Barely glancing at his daughter's wedding finery, her father went to the parlor to greet Mizushima, and they remained together absorbed in gossip about local real estate. Oshima also recognized several individuals with them being treated like family members. The partitions between rooms had been removed, and the lower-status seats, those in Mizushima's room, were already largely occupied. She heard men talking in loud, thick voices.

Heavily powdered young women paraded in and out to gossip with Oshima as she waited for the time of the ceremony. She had spoken to most of these young women at least once or twice, but none were close friends; they had been hired to serve at the reception after the ceremony. Among them were Tokyo women wearing the latest fashions with their obi tied squeaky tight.

As the young women began serving dinner on individual trays, Aoyagi's wife and the hairdresser at last led Oshima out to the bride's seat facing the guests at the front of the room.

"Your turn for the bridal veil has finally come," Aoyagi remarked playfully to Oshima, whose heart was pounding. At first she refused to wear the floss silk veil, but Aoyagi had insisted, and their discussion became quite heated before Oshima allowed the garment to be placed over her face.

The marriage ceremony consisted of the exchange of nuptial cups of sake. Three times the bride drank from the cup, which was then refilled for the bridegroom, who in turn drank three times. When the ceremony was finished, Oshima, as if fleeing, rushed back to her own room. She was not permitted to remove the veil until she returned.

On changing into a new kimono for the reception and going back to the ceremony room, she was confronted by a sea of faces, and it was only after she was guided to her seat and had regained her composure that it dawned on her that Saku was the bridegroom at her wedding. Dressed in newly made *haori* and *hakama,* he looked ill at ease seated in formal posture. He glanced quickly at her with frightened eyes.

Blood rose to Oshima's head in a fit of rage. The moving figures of the serving girls under the lights seemed to swirl before her eyes. She sat very still, her head bowed, and was overcome by an uncontrollable shivering.

"How about it, Oshima?" Aoyagi asked, leaning over to look up at her face. "From this perspective, he doesn't appear a complete fool, does he?" His soft, personal tone seemed to patronize her, increasing her rage.

Saku, clumsily sipping his soup, laughed obsequiously.

For the first time, Oshima realized how terrifying were the actions and words of adults. The sight of Saku hungrily wolfing down his food made her flesh crawl, and then her entire body was suddenly shaking. Pale as a sheet, she rose and walked unsteadily out of the room.

By the time a few individuals caught up with Oshima in her room, she was undressing as if in a dream.

22

THEY TRIED AT LENGTH to coax Oshima back to the ceremony, but she sat on the floor clinging to the open sliding doors of her closet. She would not budge.

"I give up," Aoyagi declared, appalled by Oshima's obstinacy after trying any number of times to pry her fingers loose from the doors. Aoyagi was replaced by Nishida and Oshima's natural father, who together pulled Oshima into the middle of the room and alternately threatened and cajoled in low voices.

"I told you to trust me. If you go on acting like this, you'll ruin the whole plan," Nishida complained bitterly.

"I'll go back to the ceremony. Just give me a moment to recover." Oshima finally wiped the tears from her face and smiled.

"We all know you hate him. But you have to see this through. You lose by any other strategy. Just keep telling yourself, I'm marrying the property, and you won't lose your temper," Nishida cautioned before he left the room.

The reception, grown quiet and sober since Oshima's departure, livened up again. Guests who had come to look in on Oshima returned to their seats, and the women serving the sake became very busy.

Saku passed the entrance to Oshima's room and caught sight of her in the dim light. "What's wrong, Oshima? No need to be so sensitive." Oshima, her obi undone, was seated with her back against the door of her closet and her head buried in her arms. Her beautiful coiffure had collapsed at the center during her crazed outburst of rage. Oshima felt Saku's hot breath smelling of sake against her cheek and then his hand attempting to fondle her breast.

"What're you doing!" the startled Oshima exclaimed, suddenly sitting up straight, and she brought the flat of her open hand down hard, with a stinging sound, against Saku's cheek.

"Oh! That's a mean thing to do," Saku declared, glaring at Oshima with resentment as he held his cheek.

The hairdresser came and redid Oshima's hair and makeup. By the time Oshima appeared again at the reception, the celebration was disintegrating into drunken revelry. Aoyagi, intoxicated to the point of mindlessness, pulled Oshima over by Saku and made her sit down. Oshima's father and Mizushima were no longer present. Sake was being forced on Saku by four or five young men who surrounded him. With his vacant eyes, gaping mouth, and sad-looking physique, he appeared all the more pathetic to Oshima.

23

AT THE FIRST LIGHT of dawn, Oshima checked the regular breathing of Sakutarō, who had collapsed in a drunken sleep, and, a little later, the last of the young men still celebrating fell silent in an exhausted slumber. Oshima ran out of the house.

She washed off her caking face powder in the well and proceeded up the path between the rice paddies in back. The farmhouses at the edges of groves of trees were outlined in the mist, and the first cooking fires of the day flickered in the darkness. She saw shadowy figures hunched against the cold on their way to work in the rice paddies. The screech of a cart being pulled on the damp path echoed in the silence. Dawn's breeze felt clean against Oshima's cheeks, which were as hot as a feverish patient's. She hurried along the path through the wild fields. Oshima had not slept at all during the night, and she felt dirty, as though Saku's face, reeking of sake, and his gruesome bony limbs were still being forced on her.

The sun had risen by the time Oshima reached the outskirts of Ōji. Smoke from cooking fires curled up from most of the houses. She heard the jumbled sounds of the town waking up.

"I'll bet there's a commotion back at Ogu now," she thought with satisfaction as she approached the rear entrance of her sister's house, which was located at the edge of the town.

Peering through the rough bamboo hedge, Oshima spotted her sister carrying her child on her back and washing diapers at the well surrounded by the dainty white flowers of a thriving sasanqua bush. Her husband, once an employee in her father's house, was ladling water on ornamental garden bushes by a field of flowers. In her confused mind, Oshima envied the impoverished life led by the couple working together only for each other. Her sister married this poor laborer because she wanted him. Their fields were planted thick with the plum and pine trees that would be taken to town for sale in the spring. Morning sunlight glinted on the earth. The well rope creaked lazily as the bucket moved up and down.

"I won't stay long. I'll leave in a day or two," Oshima pleaded, seeking refuge with her sister. She immediately tried to be of use, pulling up water, splashing it over the soapy diapers, and wringing them out.

"You think that's a good idea? In the end, you'll just apologize and go back to them anyway," the sister declared, swaying left to right, rocking the baby on her back as she gazed down at Oshima working energetically in front of her.

"Never! Whatever happens, this time I'm not going back!" Oshima insisted.

She took the diapers that she had wrung out over to a bamboo pole, suspended to take full advantage of the warmth of the sun. As she hung up the diapers, the strong sunlight pierced her damp, swollen eyes. Her head began to ache.

"Oshima's run away again!" the sister shouted to her husband.

The husband, ladle in hand, gazed at Oshima and began laughing. Brushing the tears from her dazzled eyes, Oshima started laughing, too.

24

TO SCOUT OUT the situation for Oshima, her sister visited her parents' house that evening. When she arrived, people sent to search for Oshima were talking to her father. Her mother was preparing food and sake in the kitchen to placate the angry guests. After chatting with her mother in the kitchen, the sister returned and reported to Oshima.

"Oshima, you should at least pay your respects before they leave," her sister advised. Oshima had suffered from a headache the whole day and was resting in bed.

Oshima's chest contracted in irritation. Tonight she would find some money and run away to her brother's place, far off in the provinces. Losing herself in fantasy, she imagined crossing over to a foreign land by ship and merging with the laboring masses. She still felt pain in some of her joints, the result of her fierce resistance against Saku the night before.

Her sister's husband as well urged Oshima to visit her parents. Oshima half dismissed their tiresome suggestions, but she knew that she could not hold out against them for long.

"Mother and father don't understand me. They're ganging up with the rest of them, forcing me to do what they want," Oshima muttered angrily as she left.

Outside, night had fallen. The electric lights of the Yamanote train line and lanterns from individual dwellings glowed fresh through the deep, rising mist. Quiet had descended on the elegant residences bordering the tea fields.

Oshima arrived at her natural parents' house shortly after the departure of those sent to find her. Appearing before her mother and father, her breathing grew rapid and shallow, and her resolve of the previous night weakened.

"I'm sorry I caused you trouble. Please forgive me!" she said, attempting to bow, but her muscles were so stiff she could barely lower her head.

"What idiot act have you disgraced us with this time?" Enraged, her father would not allow his daughter to defend herself. At last Oshima understood her father's true intent: he would close his eyes to just about anything to gain control of Mizushima's wealth.

25

AT THE END OF NUMEROUS negotiations, Oshima agreed to return to her foster parents. She left her natural parents one evening in the company of Aoyagi.

Her defiance had driven her natural parents to despair. She so angered her normally gentle father that he resorted to violence, grabbing her by the hair, twisting her to the floor, and raining blows down on her. Calls for Oshima's punishment had reached him from several acquaintances who had negotiated for her return. According to these sources, her behavior made it difficult for her foster parents to entrust their property to her. One spoke of her carelessness with money and her too easy generosity. Another testified that Oshima told Mizushima about his wife's secret affair with Aoyagi in an attempt to create domestic turmoil. In the end, however, the chief complaint against her was Mizushima's disappointment at her lack of resolve to persevere with her foster family in times of adversity.

"I told you so. I've kept an eye on her since she was a child. I've always known she was no good. I'm certain the Mizushimas lost all affection for her long ago! They'd have kicked her out if she hadn't left." Oshima's natural mother continued, recalling how obstinate her daughter was as a girl, and she cursed the weak sentimentality of her husband, clinging to a semblance of love for his daughter.

"Who'd be fool enough to trust that juvenile delinquent with fifty or a hundred thousand yen of their property?" The mother gained tremendous satisfaction in humiliating Oshima before her younger sister and brother. She was able to avenge herself on her husband, who had protected his daughter in secret for many years. Oshima was sulking and refused to come in to dinner.

But Oshima was not to be defeated. She entered and showered her mother with language so abusive that the woman began shaking and the veins stood out on her harsh, square face. Bringing up each of the cruelties that she had suffered as a child at her mother's hand caused tears to flow down Oshima's cheeks. She felt herself surrender to an inconsolable sadness.

"Bitch!" "Drop dead!" "Unfilial daughter!" "Devil!" "Child killer!"—words of the most vitriolic kind were exchanged by the two angry women.

At the end of this fight, Aoyagi stepped in and deftly convinced Oshima to accompany him back to her foster family. Once again, she stormed out of her natural parents' home.

26

THERE WAS NO MOON in the clear night sky. Stars twinkled randomly in the vast Milky Way. A pale mist crawled up from the earth. Oshima was startled by the sound of water rustling at her feet, then found herself surrounded by the fog it raised. She wondered how she had been capable of the continuous battle with her mother for the past few days, a fight that roused her as if to madness and exhausted the last of her strength. From time to time, she raised her head to the sky and sighed. The road entered dim stands of trees with no signs of human life, then rose to the top of a high embankment along railroad tracks. Oshima noticed steel rails glittering below and heard insects chirping in the thick grass on the embankment. If Aoyagi had not been with her, she would have thrown herself down in the grass and cried her heart out.

She did not walk much further in Aoyagi's company. They passed under a large pine on a hill cluttered with old gravestones and stone images of Jizō, the protective deity of children. Then Aoyagi's intention to gratify himself, which she had sensed before, finally took concrete form.

"Stop it! You're joking, right?" she declared laughing as she brushed aside his exploring hands and strode off. Aoyagi caught up with her and attempted to seduce her with romantic words.

"Mother will scold you," she said, trying to dodge his advances with humor.

"What help do you think she'll be to you? I have complete control over the affairs of your family. I can have your name taken out of the family registry and send it where I choose, or I can keep you safe in the family. I can do with you what I please!" he declared.

Oshima put up a protracted physical struggle, exasperating the man with her defiance and violence before she was able to escape and dash to the public road.

She ran panting back to the house of her natural parents and rushed into her father's bedroom.

"If your story's true, I'll have something to say about it," her father, who had been asleep, declared. Sitting up in his bedding as he smoked, he considered Oshima's account of the incident.

"That's the kind of animal he is. He certainly misjudged me!" Oshima said indignantly, pushing back her disheveled hair. In a lively manner, she proceeded to exaggerate the description of the scene of battle with Aoyagi. That she seemed to be winning back her father's trust and getting the better of her mother put Oshima in a good mood.

27

THE RICKSHA PULLER, an elderly man named Gin who was a beneficiary of Oshima's largesse, arrived to take Oshima back to her foster parents shortly after she and her father had gone to bed. He would not say who sent him.

"What can it be at this hour?" she wondered, going out in her nightgown to open the gate for the man. On New Year's Day and the Festival of Souls in the summer, Oshima always bought Gin's children gifts of clothing or had rice cakes made for them. Now, he refused to leave, for, he said, returning without her that night would put his family in disfavor with Mizushima.

"I'm certain Aoyagi talked it over with Otora and they sent him," Oshima concluded with a wry laugh in her brief report to her father. Learning from Oshima about the scandalous incidents that occurred in the foster family plainly disturbed her father, but he was not quite resigned to taking his daughter back as the situation stood. It was the first he had heard of Otora's promise that, if Oshima married Saku-tarō, she would be free to pursue her own secret desires.

"She told me several times she wouldn't mind if I bought myself an actor or took a lover. She'd understand because she'd done the same thing. I'm certain she did far worse things when she was young," Oshima said, inciting her old-fashioned father.

Judging from what had just happened to his daughter, her father seemed convinced that it was dangerous to leave her in the midst of that gang, and he decided to bring Oshima back into the family. But, with the arrival of the ricksha puller, his resolve weakened.

In the end, he agreed that Oshima would return to her foster parents that night. With Oshima safely seated in his ricksha, Gin picked up the shafts of the vehicle. "Everyone says you ran off because you hate Saku. It's the talk of the whole neighborhood. But, if you leave, you'll only hurt yourself. You'll regret letting outsiders get their hands on that property!"

"I'd like to see the expression on that dumb Saku's face about now," Oshima laughed from her seat high above Gin.

On her return to her foster parents' home, Oshima did not feel like apologizing and bowing in front of her foster father as she usually did, and she went straight to her room and hurriedly prepared to go to bed.

"If she's returned, why can't she come in and pay her respects?" Oshima heard Mizushima's booming, angry voice as though he were next to her.

"You're in the wrong again," Otora lectured Oshima. Oshima, in her nightgown, had been summoned into her foster parents' room and was seated at the head of her foster mother's bedding.

"You take off your clothes and go to sleep without folding and putting them away. That's why your father insists he won't let you inherit his property."

The defiant Oshima made her foster father so angry that he beat her with a rolling pin and kicked her when she was down.

28

IN THE SPRING of the following year, with the enthusiastic encouragement of her mother and father, Oshima married her betrothed, a canner in the Kanda ward. A member of her father's guild, the retired head of the gardening family Uegen, acted as the intermediary. Long negotiations with the Mizushimas were required before Oshima was permitted to take away some of her clothing and hair ornaments. This wedding was not a gay event.

Oshima's husband was named Tsuru. He was born in Uegen's hometown and worked diligently for the owner of the canner's shop. Building up experience and connections in the city by making the rounds of customers, he also spent nearly two years in a cannery in Hokkaido, where he worked and slept with the laborers. His years of devoted service were rewarded by marriage to the owner's daughter, and he subsequently inherited the shop, but his wife was sickly and had died in the autumn of the previous year. He was almost ten years older than Oshima.

Tsuru was well acquainted with Oshima's older sister. The eldest son's wife at Uegen, Oyū, the daughter of a master carpenter in Kanda, was also familiar with Tsuru, and she gossiped about him constantly. Her parents' home was close to the canner's shop, so she had known the pale, gentle-mannered Tsuru long before he became his master's adopted heir. In those days, he wore an English-style hunting cap and rode a bicycle as he made the rounds of Western restaurants and the kitchens of wealthy families to take orders for imported foods and the goods that his business canned.

Until almost the date of the wedding, Oshima was not aware that her bridegroom's former wife had died of lung disease. Learning of the cause of death from an inadvertent remark by her sister made Oshima uneasy.

"I've heard Tsuru's had enough of slender, delicate women and he wants a wife who's strong and a hard worker. You certainly fit the bill there," her sister said, teasing the full-figured, robust Oshima. Oshima felt that her sister was jealous of her good fortune in marrying the handsome Tsuru. Her sister also envied Oshima's possession of the dead wife's two chests of clothes, left as they were upstairs in Tsuru's house.

Until the ceremonial exchange of betrothal gifts, when the list of presents was formally displayed, Oshima's instinctive reaction against authority caused her to believe that the proposed marriage, forced on her by outsiders, was leading to a dark future. She could not give herself over to the innocent satisfaction and joy that many young women embraced at the prospect of marriage. It made her feel small, wounded her pride and undercut her sense of dominance in relationships to people associated with her foster family. Rumors that Saku had taken a wife reached her during the year. Nishida had mentioned it, and so had another acquaintance from the region. Oshima knew the woman, the masculine-looking daughter of a local farmer.

"I should go see how the fool's getting on," Oshima commented, laughing, but she was angered by her mother's comparing her poorly to the woman, as if it were possible to compare her with Saku's new bride.

29

THE DAY AFTER the wedding, Tsuru was up early and at work with his apprentice down in the shop. Oshima and Tsuru had concluded an informal marriage ceremony the night before with only a few close friends and family. The bridegroom's formal coat and the bride's underskirt and crested kimono were scattered around the small second-floor room. Gifts were still piled in profusion about the center wedding decoration.

The last of the guests departed, and Tsuru took off his coat, the one new piece of clothing that he had had made for the ceremony. Then he went down twice to check the doors and look around the shop. On his return, Oshima was sitting by the bedding, which someone had taken down and spread out. He suddenly began talking to her about his business and property. He also complained of the hardships of caring for his former wife during her long illness, of all he had done, looking after her in the hospital or taking her to the sea, and the enormous expense. The cannery in Hokkaido, which had been founded by his father-in-law, was supervised by a competent, trustworthy manager, but Tsuru felt obliged to travel there at least once a year during times he could spare from expanding his sales network in Tokyo. Then Oshima would have to look after the shop and be vigilant in protecting her husband's interests. Since he knew that she had experience in business and sales, he had great hopes for her.

The following day passed quickly because Oshima was hard at work straightening up after the wedding. Upstairs, she often drifted over to the window and gazed through the wooden slats at the street below: across the way, there was a cosmetics shop, a shop selling geta, and a shop specializing in cotton knit goods. But Oshima could not bear remaining cooped up in that small room as cramped as a cell. She went downstairs and saw that the eaves of the neighboring house almost touched Tsuru's shop, allowing only faint sunlight into the room off the kitchen. This space as well was crowded with boxes. In the shop, a young man wearing a canvas apron was seated in the cashier's area. Tsuru was seated there, too, and he was alternately looking over his books and reading a newspaper. Oshima tried sitting passively next to her husband, but she felt uncomfortable.

Several days passed. Oshima had her hair done in the manner of a respectable young wife and became more accustomed to sitting in the cashier's area. Tsuru spent half the day out on his bicycle, making the rounds of customers. At night he was tired and went up to bed early. Oshima thought it strange that most of the day she seemed to be waiting for the sun to set. Was Tsuru as attractive as her sister and the wife of Uegen's young master claimed, she wondered, gazing at him from time to time as he worked in the cashier's area. Alone, she nurtured warm thoughts of him. She concluded that her heart was being won over by her new husband.

30

WITH THE FINE SPRING WEATHER, Tsuru decided to take a day off. He wanted to thank Uegen for acting as the go-between for the marriage. He proposed that they pay respects to Oshima's parents as well. Oshima's presence would also be required for a visit to his former wife's half brother, a canner in Yotsuya who was the son of Tsuru's deceased father-in-law by a certain woman—whether a mistress or a maidservant it was not clear. But that was purely a business matter and could wait. Tsuru could not stand the half brother's mother, and he decided to postpone that visit.

Oshima, finally grown used to her conservative hairstyle, thought a red chignon hair band did not match her rather severe features, so she replaced it with a softer orangish one. She was smearing white liquid makeup on her neck to cover her somewhat rough skin when it occurred to her that she did not know what to wear.

Tsuru seemed embarrassed by Oshima's huge hairdo and her countrified heavy makeup, and he could not find in her wardrobe a kimono conservative enough to satisfy him.

"Take a look at Kane's clothes. There might be something suitable," he suggested. Rummaging around in the drawer of a chest in the closet, Tsuru threw the jingling set of keys next to Oshima.

"Do you think it's proper for me to wear your dead wife's clothing on our first visit?"

"I suppose you're right," he replied with a sad smile.

"And if your wife remains attached to these clothes in the next life, I'll be in trouble," she continued as she went through her own drawers. "Still, I'd like to see the beautiful kimonos your wife owned."

"The old woman from Yotsuya came and took many of them away," Tsuru said in a tone suggesting his hatred of the half brother's mother. "The greedy witch started hauling stuff out of the house even before Kane died. She'd make excuses like the pattern of this kimono is out of fashion or that one's more suitable for an elderly woman," he went on, not bothering to conceal his frustration and regret.

Oshima unlocked the chest, pulled out several of the drawers, and held up one kimono after another, but, in her view, most seemed too dowdy. There were few that she wished to try on.

"If she's so desperate for a few clothes, you might as well give them all to her. That'll put an end to it."

"I'd rather sell them to a used clothing dealer."

Tsuru and Oshima went out together for the first time. Tsuru strode on ahead through the neighborhood and, after walking half a block, turned and looked over his shoulder. Oshima was hurrying to catch up, each long, reaching step revealing a flash of underskirt. She had spread her cream-colored parasol to protect her from the sun. A warm spring breeze lightly swirled up sand from the street, and branches of the willow bent gracefully under the weight of young leaves that had appeared suddenly, as if by magic. Oshima's heart was dancing in elation. She was jubilant over her debut in this bright society, which she had never experienced before, but her happiness was clouded by moments of self-doubt and sadness, for she knew she had not yet fathomed the depths of her husband's heart. Oshima's kindness and benevolence to others had been remarkable enough to occasion criticism from her foster mother and father, and she herself took pride and satisfaction in her own generosity, yet she had never before felt that she could love a person with her whole heart. No one had ever truly loved her either. She wanted to love Tsuru, but it seemed that the ghost of Tsuru's dead wife still occupied his heart. Oshima also believed he treasured the memory of his wife and had married her only to obtain a helper in life. On board the tram with her new husband, she continued to be troubled by these thoughts.

31

THE UEGEN FAMILY had been well-known in the Kanda ward for many years. The family's harshness to apprentices was so notorious that it gave rise to the local saying, "Go into service at Uegen, or get a job bearing bundles of thorns on your bare back—they're both about the same." Different from the family of gardeners Oshima was born into, the Uegens once lived extravagantly. Now the retired mistress of the house was elderly and had relaxed her strict rules for conducting the household and business. Oshima had previously visited a few times but had never been invited into the house.

Oyū, the wife of Uegen's eldest son and the daughter of the carpenter Daimasa, had been Tsuru's friend since his apprentice days, and Tsuru greeted her in a familiar way. Their seeming fondness for each other created an unfavorable impression, though this was the first time Oshima had had a good look at Oyū.

Oshima had heard from her sister that Oyū was a flirt, but, on meeting her, Oshima found a graceful woman, easy and assured, perhaps because of her training in the traditional musical arts. The hairline at her forehead was a perfect triangle, the shape of Mount Fuji, although the forehead was too small. Her eyes were long and narrow, her mouth slightly too large, but her fine skin was pure white, and Oshima thought her small figure beautifully proportioned. Tsuru seemed at ease in the house and was about to enter the family room, littered with sewing, when Oyū stopped him, saying that it was no place to receive guests; instead, she led them to the front of the alcove in the main room and put down cushions, side by side, for the couple to sit on. Tsuru moved his cushion away from Oshima and sat down.

"There's no need to treat me like a formal guest," Tsuru objected.

"At your age, you shouldn't feel shy in these social situations," Oyū said, blushing as she compared the new husband and wife.

"Have you grown used to your new home?" she asked, turning to Oshima.

"I'm a clumsy sort of person, as you see. I'm afraid I'm constantly being scolded," Oshima countered diplomatically.

"But the neighborhood's interesting. There's so much happening around you," Oyū said, staring at Oshima's hairstyle and patting her own hair with her hand.

The fidgety Tsuru could not sit still, and he went out to look at the garden and pay his respects to the retired mistress of the house. Oyū was restless as well, and she drew close to Tsuru from time to time as she joked and laughed. Dozens of large pots containing rosebushes were in rows in front of the greenhouse. Red and purple Western flowers were placed on shelves outside to air. Sightseers in small groups around the summerhouse wandered among the young men working there.

"It's getting late," Tsuru said to Oshima as he looked at his watch. "I won't get back in time if I visit your parents. Maybe you should go on by yourself."

"That won't do!" Oyū declared as she refilled her guests' tea bowls.

It was decided that Tsuru and Oshima would leave together. For Oshima, the excursion was proving a disappointment.

32

CLOUDS WERE MOVING across the sun, and the couple regarded the half-mile walk before them as an arduous chore. It was obvious to Oshima that Tsuru's main purpose that day had been to visit Uegen. Whatever interest he had in meeting her parents had disappeared, for he seemed on the verge of returning home. She was indignant because she had been dragged along just to witness Tsuru's relationship with his old friend and forced to observe that Tsuru was happier and more carefree when talking with Oyū than he was with her alone. She did not feel that he was displeased with her, but they were not walking together with the same intimacy as they had at the beginning of the day.

"It's not right to come this far and not pay them a visit!" Tsuru objected in response to Oshima's suggestion that they return home. Tsuru revealed a conservative merchant's streak in deciding to press on and not waste the trip and the rest of the day.

"You don't have to go for my sake. They don't consider me their daughter, and I don't consider them my parents. I was born in their house, but they're not really my family," she said as she followed him.

Only her mother was at home. The attitudes of Oshima and her mother were so hardened toward each other that the mother could not feign affection for her daughter, even for the sake of a son-in-law she had never met. When alone with Tsuru, however, the mother's demeanor softened. Afraid that her mother was disparaging her, Oshima lingered at the entrance to overhear their conversation. Tsuru showed a more personable side and tried to win the woman over. He chattered on about how he suffered before he was adopted by his father-in-law and how hard he worked, burdened with a sick wife, building up his business.

"Oshima and I must work as one to keep profits up, or we won't survive."

Tsuru paid no notice when Oshima sat next to him, and, from Oshima's perspective, this indifference endeared him to her mother.

"Please come visit us at the shop," Tsuru invited, in the spirit of their amiable conversation.

What's he talking about? Oshima thought. The entire visit seemed ridiculous. She turned away and gazed outside, interrupting occasionally to mention that it was time to leave.

"She's such an impatient child. I'm certain she'll cause you trouble. Be strict with her! Scold her, and get as much work out of her as you can," her mother insisted, glaring at Oshima.

Tsuru continued speaking as if he were deeply moved by Oshima's mother's concern. At last he put away his pipe and prepared to leave.

"Why were you agreeing with her? Mother understands nothing about business. She works people to death like horses or oxen!" the irritated Oshima complained once she and Tsuru were on the street.

33

ON A DAY DURING the hottest part of summer, Tsuru suddenly decided he would travel to Hokkaido. Once the impetuous Tsuru had made the decision to leave, he could scarcely wait for dawn. In the morning, carrying a change of clothing in his bag, a briefcase, a lap robe, and his cigarette pouch, Tsuru left the house in the company of his apprentice, who was to see him off at the station. Tsuru's manner was that of a holiday vacationer with no final destination in mind. Having mastered her husband's business during the four months that she had lived with him, Oshima was entrusted with complete responsibility for the shop in his absence. Dressed in a fashionable white kimono tied loosely with a broad sash of striped silk and wearing a panama hat, Tsuru cut a dashing figure as he departed. When she saw him off at the entrance of the shop, Oshima experienced a loneliness she had never felt before.

Earlier that month, as the month before, Oshima had missed her period, normally so regular, and this confirmed her suspicions. But she had felt confident enough to mention it only the previous night, after Tsuru had finished his hurried preparations for the journey.

"Something peculiar's happening to my body. I think it's—you know," she announced, sitting by the drowsing Tsuru when she returned from the toilet.

The summer night was humid, and, shortly after the clock struck ten, she heard the clattering footsteps of people still passing in front of the shop. Tsuru always went to bed early and woke up at dawn.

"It's too soon for that. Sounds suspicious!" Tsuru declared, with a skeptical glance. He extended his white, supple arm to draw his ashtray near. Recently, he had made the trip to the local municipal office to recognize Oshima as his wife legally by putting her name in his family registry, but, in doing so, he had discovered that she had once been married to Sakutarō, at least technically. He felt betrayed and had determined to divorce his new wife. But Tsuru lacked the courage to announce his intention to all those concerned. Instead, he hinted at his resentment by making occasional sly digs or disagreeable remarks, venting his frustration on Oshima. From about that time, Oshima often smelt sake on Tsuru's breath when he returned from making the rounds of customers. She also began intercepting telephone calls for Tsuru from a gentle-voiced woman. Oshima imitated the voice of the shop's young male apprentice in a strained attempt to learn the name of the caller, but her efforts were fruitless. She was tortured by jealous doubts about what Tsuru might be up to while supposedly making the rounds of customers. Maybe his lover was Uegen's young wife, Oyū, or perhaps her own sister— she suspected even those closest to her. The women who praised Tsuru were judged by Oshima to be rivals in love.

Oshima's sister would come and spend half the day visiting. Once Tsuru teasingly praised her appearance, and she replied, "Then why didn't you marry me?" She seemed half serious, half joking, and completely unconcerned that Oshima was present. But she was blushing as she asked the question.

Oshima found her sister's words so offensive that they later became the cause of a quarrel between Tsuru and herself.

34

RETURNING HOME, his face red with drink, Tsuru delighted in questioning Oshima about the most intimate details of her life before she married him. Oshima's descriptions of Sakutarō briefly relieved Tsuru's doubts about her former marriage, but his suspicions returned much as a crushed rubber ball regains its former shape.

"If you think I'm lying, then go to my foster family and see for yourself. 'They made her marry a man like that'—that's what you'll think. How can I describe him to you!" Oshima seemed to tremble with revulsion as she spoke of Saku.

"Whether you hated him or not isn't the point. The fact is you married him!" Tsuru declared.

"My foster parents must have done it. I never dreamed they officially registered my name in marriage."

"Isn't it strange that you're registered in your husband's household, not with Mizushima?"

She had not paid much attention to the problem of her registry at first, but, after Tsuru mentioned it several times, she vaguely became aware of her foster parents' true intent in forcing Sakutarō on her.

"Then they never had any intention of letting me inherit their property!" Oshima felt immense disappointment. She had been convinced for so long that her foster parents and those around them placed their trust in her alone. Now her confidence in herself was shaken to its core. She remembered the many statements and actions by which people assured her that she would be the heiress.

"Bastards! I won't rest until I have it out with them," she thought, but, in her heart, she was as much angered by her own gullibility in working ceaselessly to please her cruel foster mother. Most of all, she regretted that Tsuru might regard her as promiscuous.

Hints from the shop's apprentice informed Oshima that Tsuru was meeting clandestinely with a Shitaya woman whom he had known during the two years of his former wife's illness. At times, Oshima would give the apprentices small gifts of money or treat them to meals. On occasion, they were stung by fits of rage from their aggressive woman boss, but more often they were surprised by her generosity.

Oshima made the rounds of the customers, too, leaving after Tsuru, and there were nights when Oshima and Tsuru returned together late, on friendly terms, both bearing gifts for everyone in the shop.

35

BURNED BY THE ROUGH SUMMER WIND, Tsuru returned home from Hokkaido about two and a half months later. The worst heat of August had passed, and breezes cooled the air in the mornings and evenings as autumn clouds moved across the sky over Tokyo. According to Tsuru, his return was delayed because he had stopped by his hometown in the northeast to see his aging father. There he fell ill and was forced to recover at a local hot-spring resort. It was not difficult for Oshima to see through this fabrication when a letter from a woman whom he had met on his trip arrived for Tsuru while he was out.

Without telling Oshima one story about his journey, Tsuru went back to his work, most of it outside the shop, but, going over his books one day, he discovered that, while on her own initiative Oshima expanded his business network substantially, most of the new customers were not paying their bills. He recognized several families who had cheated him before, but there were also reputable people, old acquaintances of Oshima's. In his absence, it seemed Oshima's daily work was soliciting orders from anyone with whom she had even the slightest connection, and, in case after case, he found that the merchandise had been delivered and payment not received.

During the summer, there were many occasions when Oshima suffered severe morning sickness, and she would spend all day upstairs in bed without coming down to the shop. Even when she felt well, she would often tire of counting up daily receipts or figuring out end-of-the-month billings with the apprentices, and she would dress up and amuse herself by visiting her natural family, or Uegen's, or going to gossip with her foster family's customers and associates. She was still on friendly terms with many of them. Sakutarō had been set up with his bride in a small apartment in a tenement close to Mizushima's house. As always, he and his wife were being worked half to death.

"I thought I'd buy a cheap present and go see your new husband," Saku said with a broad, silly grin.

"Just keep working hard for happiness in the next life. You won't find it in this one. I was almost deceived by them, too. Our foster mother and the rest are evil people!" she exclaimed as a parting line and returned home.

36

OSHIMA'S SISTER CAME to visit for the first time in months, and she gossiped at length about Tsuru, absent from the shop for the day, and about Uegen's young wife. Oshima did not want to hear about Oyū.

After a difficult pregnant customer departed, the exhausted Oshima leaned against the railing around the cashier's area and stared into space. Her pregnancy had progressed to the point where it was embarrassing to cool herself at the front of the shop in the evenings while the weather still called for single-layered, light clothing.

Since his return from Hokkaido, Tsuru spent little time balancing accounts in the cashier's area. On the rare occasions when he stayed at home during the day, he went upstairs in the morning, brought out his pillow, and lay down. In good humor, he sang obscene songs that Oshima had never heard before.

Oshima, sitting next to him, giggled nervously. "Who taught you that?" she inquired, fingering a piece of the infant's clothing she had recently begun sewing. "Love songs of Hokkaido women are too sentimental!"

Tsuru seemed about to say something but instead stared in wonder at the infant's undergarment that was taking shape.

"Who do you think the baby'll look like when it's born?" Oshima asked Tsuru the question often on her mind recently.

"It won't resemble me. You can be certain of that!" Tsuru replied with a snort and turned his back on his wife.

"No, it won't. It's a little present I've brought with me," she answered back, blushing in displeasure. "Even as a joke, that's a cruel thing to say. It's hard on the child."

"The child's hard on me!" he replied.

"Why? Because you won't be able to see your whores?"

The nerves of the couple were severely frayed. Weeping, Oshima attacked Tsuru, and he sprang to his feet, picked up the briefcase he almost never opened at home, and flew out of the house. The briefcase was filled with photographs and letters from women.

When she first heard the stories from her sister, Oshima had paid scant attention, but now each seemed to hold deep significance, and she anxiously recalled what she had been told. According to her sister, Tsuru showed Oyū the love letters he kept in the briefcase he always carried. Oyū and he read them together.

"It's a strange thing to do," the sister said, in part to incite Oshima, in part because of her own jealousy of Oyū's friendship with Tsuru.

"Tsuru's whore," she continued enthusiastically, "drifted to Hokkaido from Echigo, famous, you know, for beautiful women, and, while your husband was in Hokkaido, he hardly showed his face at the cannery and spent all his time with her. In her letters, she even describes other affairs she's having. One's with an old man from Tokyo who acts like a big spender when he goes to Hokkaido. She says that, if he sells one of his mines, he's promised to buy out her contract of indenture and take her to Tokyo. And she asks Tsuru whether she should agree as a means to get to Tokyo. She's a whore, but she's an expensive one." Her sister reported in detail to Oshima rumors about the woman that she had heard from Oyū.

"And she says Tsuru often sends kimonos, perfume, and other expensive gifts to Hokkaido. You'd better work harder to make Tsuru happy," she added.

"Nonsense," Oshima thought at the time, but now she was fearful and uncertain about what scheme the Hokkaido woman would think up next.

37

ON THE DAY that Oshima and Tsuru had their most ferocious battle, they were in Oyū's room at Uegen's, and Oshima was dressed in the gaudiest clothing and accessories she had ever worn.

Without Tsuru's permission, Oshima charged the new clothing to his account at his clothier and came away with an expensive kimono more appropriate to the adored daughter or young wife of the nouveau riche. Dressed in her resolutely extravagant clothing, Oshima first visited her sister, who watched this new Oshima with wary eyes, fearful of what she might do next. Oshima's modified Western-style coiffure glittered with cheap jewels; and rings, which she had never worn before, decorated her fingers; and the perfume that she had poured on herself was suffocating.

Oshima customarily wore heavy makeup, and she had continued applying layers of white liquid face powder since Tsuru's return. Various bottles of makeup cluttered her mirror stand; cosmetics she wasted money on almost in despair. When she went to bed at night, her face, coated with various mysterious lotions, gleamed with an ethereal, ghastly beauty beneath the electric light.

"That's some costume. Are merchants' wives supposed to dress like that?" her sister asked as she gazed at Oshima. The sister had recently received Oshima's old decorative combs, rings, and chignon ribbons, and her attitude was respectful.

"We won't have property or a business for much longer. I'd better do as I like now, or I'll lose out in the end. Besides, Tsuru's having his fun, keeping it secret from me."

Oshima went to her sister's convinced that Tsuru was to be found at Uegen's with Oyū. Ignoring her nervous sister's attempt to stop her, she left to search him out.

Timidly entering Uegen's house, Oshima found Tsuru absorbed in conversation over tea in the parlor with Oyū's husband and his mother. Oshima presented a gift of cakes to Oyū, who was in the back doing the laundry. While they were talking, Tsuru, clutching his briefcase, came to say that he was departing.

"You don't have to leave just because Oshima's here. Why not go home together?" suggested Oyū, politely trying to mediate between husband and wife.

"Because he has a weakness for you," Oshima said, turning to hide her tears.

The couple had a brief argument.

"I want you all to hear this with Oshima present!" Tsuru declared and turned pale.

Oyū led Oshima to her room, and Tsuru followed to continue his complaints at Oshima's side.

"I suppose both of you are to blame, but I feel sorry for Tsuru," Oyū concluded, and Oshima shed large tears of regret at this betrayal.

Oshima and Tsuru squared off, slapping each other and wrestling.

There was quite a delay before Oshima's sister, who had been summoned, arrived to take Oshima home with her.

38

AT HER SISTER'S HOUSE, Oshima continued complaining about Tsuru. She was jealous of and angry at Tsuru's victory in gaining Oyū's protection. She felt the urgent need to win Tsuru back from Oyū, who was acting as if he were her man. While she was eating dinner with her sister and her husband, Oshima's mind remained with Tsuru and Oyū.

"I have to get back. I can't stay here tonight. The apprentices are waiting for me," Oshima suddenly declared as her sister was putting her children to bed under the mosquito netting. "You know Tsuru's hopeless. If I'm gone for a day, the shop'll fall apart."

"You mustn't go on another rampage," her sister cautioned as she saw Oshima off.

Oshima expressed her gratitude and left as if she had no further plans. But she sensed that Tsuru was still at Uegen's, and she could not bring herself meekly to return straight home.

It was dark outside, and quiet had descended over the neighborhood's tea fields and flowering sasanqua bushes. As if with a will of their own, her legs moved in the direction of Uegen's house. Oyū's expression as she chastised Oshima by stating her sympathy for Tsuru remained fresh in Oshima's mind. Oshima harbored dark suspicions about Oyū, Tsuru's childhood friend, who seemed more dangerous than the Hokkaido woman.

From the large stone gate with hanging lantern inscribed with Uegen's name, Oshima peered in at the house. Through tree branches arching over the stone walkway, she could see the entrance, but there was not a trace of light. She circled around the outer hedge of Chinese hawthorn and zelkova and peeked over it here and there. Nothing moved.

By the time the ricksha she had hired carried her back to the front of her own house, it was quite late.

Entering the shop to the greetings of the apprentices, she caught sight of Tsuru sitting in the cashier's area, and she was filled with a sense of relief and joy, but she could not bring herself to speak to him.

Upstairs, she found the cluttered room as she had left it, clothes scattered everywhere. Her fatigued-looking face was reflected in the uncovered mirror on top of her chest. She stood staring at her image, struck by a vague sense of anticlimax.

39

OSHIMA CAME DOWN several times, but Tsuru showed no inclination to leave the cashier's area and go upstairs. The street in front of the shop grew quieter. She heard the sounds of the apprentices closing up the shop below. By now, Tsuru would be in the room off the kitchen. Oshima's disheveled hair made her uncomfortable, and, after redoing it in a simple Japanese style, she went down and sat in the wife's customary place with her husband by the large brazier. A splitting headache overcame her, however, and, when Tsuru finally climbed the stairs, she was already in her bedding with the covers over her head.

"I'm sorry to be in bed before you. I'm not feeling well," Oshima groaned.

Tsuru got into bed and, with his long white hands, noisily rustled through the newspaper, which he had not read that day. Then he seemed to throw it aside, and Oshima thought that he was going to sleep, until she heard the click of his briefcase: he was apparently taking something out. There was silence except for the chirping of insects in the eaves over the parlor below.

Oshima was lying on her side with her back to her husband as she strained to hear what he was doing. Her eyes, unbearably heavy before, were now wide open. When the sound of a fountain pen on paper reached her, every nerve in her body focused on it, and she turned.

"What're you doing at this time of night?" she demanded.

Tsuru was startled by the sound of her voice. A few letters with lines written in a woman's hand protruded from the briefcase. He glanced in her direction and, in silence, went back to scratching sentences on the paper. Oshima stared at her husband. Then she was up, trying to grab the letter away.

"Stop fooling around," Tsuru ordered as he calmly hid the letter under his bedding, but Oshima's hands were already on his briefcase, and, by the time he wrenched it back, she was left crawling on her knees and elbows.

"We have to talk," Tsuru said, sitting up in his bed. The exhausted Oshima lay on her stomach with her face on her pillow. Tsuru had become quite excited in his struggle to force the rampaging Oshima into submission. As he smoked, he rubbed the pink wounds her nails had inflicted. Her shoulders heaving with each breath, Oshima remained resting on her stomach.

Explaining his responsibilities to the house that he was adopted into and his social position in relation to his former wife, Tsuru concluded, "With a wife like you, who does just as she pleases, I won't survive as a merchant."

"Go tell it to Oyū!" Oshima answered bitterly and rolled over on her side, turning her back to her husband once again.

40

DURING THE TIME that Oshima was being shunted back and forth between the house of her natural parents and Uegen's, while she was not certain whether she had left her husband or he was divorcing her, Tsuru's business began to disintegrate.

Maintaining his relationship with the Hokkaido woman and becoming more passionate in his affair with the woman in Shitaya, Tsuru spent so much time away from his shop that he was not aware of an apprentice embezzling payments to customers' accounts. By the time he realized he was being cheated, he had fallen deeply in debt.

"Once the child's born, I'll do a splendid job of raising it on my own," Tsuru told Oshima when he finally confronted her with his desire for a divorce, though he had brought up the issue whenever he met Oyū or her mother-in-law.

Oshima's future had been entrusted to the go-between for her marriage, the retired woman head of the household at Uegen's. Oshima had deep misgivings about this old woman's plans, but she agreed to the arrangement to escape the daily torments inflicted by her natural mother. One morning, as Oshima was crouched over the open hearth relighting the banked fire, her mother, angered by

Oshima's back talk, shoved her daughter into the fire. Oshima struck her side against the corner of the metal oven in the hearth, and this was the cause of the miscarriage of her unfortunate fetus.

Immediately after the incident, however, Oshima finished cooking the morning rice for breakfast and ate with everyone else. It was the middle of October. The smell of miso soup in the pot on the clay charcoal stove and white steam rising from the wooden rice container reminded Oshima of past autumn mornings.

Oshima's brother, Sōtarō, the eldest son, was away chasing a woman in the provinces. His absence and her father's recent ill health gave the house an air of isolated decline. In the midst of breakfast, without even crying out, Oshima suddenly lost consciousness and collapsed. She learned later that she had suffered a miscarriage seven months into her pregnancy.

Oshima did not even get a glimpse of her stillborn child before her father and Tsuru carried it off in the evening to a temple dedicated to dead infants. Oshima, her body lightened so unexpectedly, remained in bed for less than a week.

As soon as Oshima recovered her health, it was decided between her mother and Uegen's old woman, retired head of the house, that Oshima would be sent to Uegen and put to work in the kitchen and at sewing winter clothing. Oshima had no voice in the decision.

The sharp-tongued old woman at Uegen's had scolded Tsuru for his profligacy, so it was not easy for him to visit Oyū. Oyū told Oshima of Tsuru's straitened circumstances and mentioned that he might bring the Shitaya woman into his home.

"He's so far gone, there's no saving him now," Oyū concluded. It seemed even Oyū had given up on Tsuru.

41

FOR OSHIMA, accustomed to hard labor from childhood, whose strong body seemed capable of recovering from almost any illness, rough work in the fields seemed to make her happier. At last she had escaped the constant domestic strife of her difficult marriage, which had lasted just under a year, a marriage that she had found both satisfying and frustrating.

There were three large water containers at Uegen's. When too few male hands were available, it was Oshima's job to fill each to the brim and water the flower fields and various shrubs and trees. In the morning and evening, she also helped care for the two children whom Uegen's ill daughter had brought home with her. The daughter had been married to a government official working on provincial railroads. He had once been a boarder at Uegen's, and just this past summer, seven years after being transferred to the countryside, he suddenly died.

His two children spoke a rough northern dialect. Oyū disliked them, but both were fond of Oshima. When Oshima found a few minutes, she would do the little girl's hair and tie it in a ribbon, and she did not mind getting the children up and putting them to bed, bathing them, and serving them at meals.

Uegen's daughter lost the property she had taken with her at marriage, and selling her household goods in the provinces provided barely enough money to cover travel and living expenses for a short time. She would bring her suckling infant out on the veranda, sit in the sunlight with him on her lap, and watch Oshima as she worked.

"I'm surprised your body's able to move so energetically," she called out to Oshima one day. Barefoot, with her sleeves tied up, Oshima was washing each of the stones in the walkway, pausing now and then to change the water in her washbasin. For the past few days, the hot sun of an Indian summer pierced the reed awning spread over the veranda.

"I'm used to it. I've been doing this kind of work since I was a girl," Oshima replied with a smile.

"I wouldn't have thought you'd given birth to a child."

"It was scarcely seven months. I never saw it. Better that way, I suppose."

"You can't forget your husband, can you?" the woman asked.

"We had our problems, but you're right, divorce wasn't what I wanted," Oshima replied.

"Then you were in love with him."

"I suppose I was," Oshima said, blushing. "My rages destroyed the marriage, I guess. Still, I wonder why he needed so many romances. A woman spoke to him, and he fell in love. That caused all sorts of trouble. Yet he's obsessively jealous, too," Oshima continued.

"I heard you could've made the divorce much more difficult for him than you did," the woman commented.

"I'm not a geisha or a prostitute. What's the sense of dragging the marriage out? Besides, I'm tired of spineless men!" Oshima declared.

"I suppose you're right. Perhaps I should find a job," said the daughter.

"You're joking. You couldn't possibly abandon such a cute baby boy!" Oshima answered.

42

AT NIGHT, IT WAS OSHIMA'S chore to massage the back and legs of the old woman at Uegen and prepare her for bed. She also had to pacify the old woman's outbursts of rage, which arose from her sick jealousy of her son's wife.

Although there were rumors that the old woman had hired young male entertainers well into her forties, she was also obsessively devoted to her son, Fusakichi, whom she indulged in every way and who was the object of her boundless affection from an early age, at least until Oyū came as his bride. Fusakichi once suffered a brain disease resulting in frequent depression, and, while he was a well-behaved boy, his mother felt he required her constant attention. He was given no real preparation to take up the trade of gardener, and, since his mother kept him by her side in the house, he had no friends. Fusakichi was fond of paintings and at sixteen aspired to become an artist, but his mother blocked this ambition, too, and he had received almost no training in the arts.

Supervised by his mother from the time he woke up in the morning until he went to sleep at night, Fusakichi grew resentful of her relentless gaze. Oyū's father was a carpenter who did business with the gardener Uegen, and, from time to time, Fusakichi had chances to meet the carpenter's daughter. He was attracted to the innocent-looking young woman and insisted that he would take Oyū as his bride or have no one. His mother reported his words to Oyū and her father.

After they were married, however, Fusakichi was separated from Oyū and made to sleep next to his mother when she was feeling despondent, or Oyū was kept massaging the old woman's back and legs deep into the night. The couple would hear the light-sleeping mother's footsteps outside their door late at night or her angry voice complaining that they were still in bed at the break of dawn. Since her arrival, Oshima occasionally discovered Oyū weeping alone in dark corners.

Fusakichi left the gardening to the workmen and, dressed primly in his fine clothes, spent the day arranging flowers or fiddling with his paintings. The shy young man was forced to listen to scurrilous insults from his mother.

"If you believe the child that woman's carrying is yours, you're a bigger fool than I thought," his mother exclaimed.

The listless Oyū, five months pregnant, was graced with a new innocence and beauty. As the aged mother saw Oyū's fresh voluptuousness increasing daily and her diligent efforts to please Fusakichi, she became so angry she could scarcely bear the sight of Oyū.

43

OSHIMA'S SISTER, carrying on her back her child, which wore no hat to protect it from the hot sun, circled round to the garden in back to call for Oyū. Oshima was drying silk clothing on wooden frames just within the front gate. Oyū was washing her hair on the veranda of her room. Everyone else had found a cool, airy place to take a nap. Fusakichi had left for a fishpond he frequented, and his sister, Suzu, was asleep on her side on the tatami inside, her breasts exposed to suckle her youngest child. The entire house was sunk in lethargy, exhausted by the heat of the long summer day.

At the edge of a bamboo fence along a field of large, drooping sunflowers, a host of black butterflies fluttered in the air, and it seemed as if the sky were filled with black-spotted sunlight.

Oshima's sister and Oyū talked for about five minutes on the veranda, and then the sister put her child down and wiped the sweat from her forehead with her sleeve. Not bothering to do up her still damp hair, Oyū tied it with a piece of paper and left the house.

"Tsuru is somewhere around here," Oshima thought and was so annoyed that she stopped her work. She felt anger constricting her chest.

"You're an awful person," Oshima said as she drew next to her sister.

"What do you mean?" Her sister's sweating face reddened as she leaned over to show her breast to the child crawling at her feet.

"I know what's happening!"

"Strange girl. If you know, why harass me?"

"You don't think you're doing anything wrong?" Oshima insisted.

"There's no right or wrong about it. I think you're confused," her sister replied.

Making Oshima promise several times to tell no one, her sister explained how Tsuru, on the verge of bankruptcy, had come and requested that she contact Oyū for a small loan to be kept secret from Fusakichi and his mother. Oshima could scarcely believe Tsuru was in such difficulty, but the gravity of her sister's manner convinced her that it must be so.

"So the business is done for," Oshima remarked, cocking her head to the side.

"Probably. He says he might go back to the provinces."

"Like they say, 'Bring a geisha into your house, you won't last long.' He should just declare bankruptcy, then have his fun," Oshima concluded with contempt and went back to her work, but her eyes were clouded with tears. In her mind, she pictured the nervous Oyū meeting Tsuru, his face strained by the desperation of his situation.

Oyū returned shortly, and Oshima could tell from her mixed expression of boldness and anxiety that she would do just about anything for her man, Tsuru.

When Oshima's sister departed, she carried a large soft bundle that looked like it might contain a number of Oyū's expensive winter garments.

44

OSHIMA MADE SUZU promise that she would never tell anyone, and then she recounted for her what she knew of the relationship between Oyū and Tsuru. After Suzu repeated the story to the old woman, Oshima had great difficulty in protecting Oyū from the cruelties inflicted by her mother-in-law. The obsessive old woman was convinced that at last she possessed irrefutable evidence of her daughter-in-law's infidelity.

Early in the evening, Oshima calmed the old woman and coaxed her to sleep, but, as everyone in the house was preparing for bed, the old woman sat up and stared around the wide expanse of mosquito netting, as if unable to endure the rest of the long night.

She called Fusakichi to her side and berated him for indulging his wife, but, the more enraged and exasperated she became, the more Fusakichi coldly ignored her. For Fusakichi, who remembered the days when his mother socialized with young male entertainers, her pained indignation was comically hypocritical.

"And it was all for you, because I love you," his mother concluded at the end of her story of the trials she endured in raising her frail son, but Fusakichi ignored her.

"I won't live with an imbecile who can't get rid of a slut like her! I'll leave!" the mother declared.

Fusakichi, who could articulate only half his thoughts, managed to raise a few words in protest.

"I don't know whether that happened or not, but she's my wife. You should let me handle it and stay out of our business. Who brought up this rumor in the first place?"

Oshima, massaging the old woman's shoulders, felt her cheeks catch fire.

Having worked every day for next to nothing during the summer, she was tired of ingratiating herself with the old woman, something she did from long habit, and mediating between her and her son. Hot nights made sleep difficult in the old woman's room, and her own physical longing seemed to force her nerves to function in unison with Fusakichi's mother as she turned in the direction of the young couple's room at the sound of whispered conversation.

"They're getting on nicely," Oshima murmured with a chuckle and turned away.

One night, the old woman exploded. "Fusakichi, she's got you twisted around her finger. That's why you let the slut get away with it," she declared. "I'll show you tonight how to deal with Oyū. If you're too weak to handle your own wife, you should hang yourself and get it over with!"

Touched by the sight of Oyū in tears, Fusakichi went to comfort her. Her pregnancy made him love her all the more.

The old woman brought forth a strength not even Oshima could restrain, and, brandishing a straight razor, she broke away from Oshima's grasp and rushed between the couple, slashing at Oyū. Dressed in her nightgown, the barefoot Oyū dashed outside.

45

THE UEGEN HOUSE was in an uproar until after two o'clock in the morning.

Pulling the old woman away from Fusakichi, Oshima and Suzu calmed her down and settled her in bed, but even then Oshima was not allowed to rest.

"What'll we do? Will Oyū be all right?" she asked the dazed Fusakichi after a futile search for Oyū in the garden and surrounding area.

Fusakichi was pale, and his eyes filled with tears.

"I hope so, but maybe Oyū won't be coming back. She's threatened suicide before."

"I didn't know!" Oshima said, her voice trembling. "I'll find her!"

Inquiring at several houses in the neighborhood and at her sister's, Oshima next telephoned both Tsuru and Oyū's father. She returned late at night.

"You can stop worrying," she reported, out of breath in Fusakichi's room. "Oyū's safe at her father's house."

When Oshima called, the father's young wife, Oyū's stepmother, answered the phone and responded to her questions.

Everyone was asleep when Oyū's ricksha pulled up at her parents' house. Her stern old-fashioned father immediately denounced her, and she departed feeling there was no place for her on the face of the earth. In the view of Oyū's father, who remembered his daughter's flirtations before her marriage, her gift to Tsuru of her clothing to pawn was an unforgivable sin.

By the time Oyū returned to Uegen's house, Oshima was in bed. Physically tired but unable to sleep, her attention was focused on the front entrance.

In the early morning before dawn, Oyū cut off a swath of her hair at the root and attempted to throw herself in the well. Oyū had discovered the straight-edge razor taken away from the old woman and left on the mirror stand in Oyū's room. To spite her mother-in-law and her father and gain the sympathy of Fusakichi, Oyū, without a word to her husband, who sat drowsily in his bedding, impulsively severed a handful of her undone hair. "I'll die! They've disgraced me, and I want to die!" she shouted as she struggled frantically with Oshima, who had dashed out barefoot to intercept her in the garden.

Oshima and Fusakichi at last managed to lead Oyū back into the house. Oshima felt both affection for and jealousy toward the prone woman weeping in front of her. Oyū's black hair flowed in disorder down her back.

"She wanted to prove her love for Tsuru," Oshima murmured as she compared Fusakichi, placating his wife in a gentle voice, and the beautiful Oyū, lost in tears, deaf to her husband.

46

AT THE END OF THE SUMMER, Sōtarō, Oshima's oldest brother, took Oshima to a provincial town deep in the mountains. He needed her help to establish a gardening and nursery business there. Sōtarō had been leading a rootless life following his lover as she drifted from place to place in the provinces.

"How long does mother intend to keep me working at that place?" Oshima complained to her father during a brief visit home. Oshima was tired of the hard labor and ceaseless domestic squabbles at Uegen's.

Her father brought her home to take the place of Sōtarō, who had been away from his family for many years. But Oshima was won over by her brother, who had returned to acquire provisions and stock for the new business, and, on an impulse, she decided to accompany him back to the mountains. Sōtarō had decided to start his business there in the first place because his woman was being kept nearby as the mistress of another man.

"It's a hard life, and not everyone can make it, but I know you can," her brother declared, urging her. Oshima was both insecure living with her natural family and attracted to the prospect of adventure. She was thus susceptible to the persuasions of her brother.

At the station, Sōtarō supervised the loading of a large stock of garden trees and bushes and Western-style flower seeds that he planned to wholesale to other gardeners. Then he boarded the train. Oshima, seated next to him, was imagining the provincial town, which she had never seen, and, as the train pulled out, she felt great relief. In all the places she had been before—with her cruel mother, her hard-hearted foster parents, the old woman at Uegen's—Oshima had been victimized and exploited, and the mere thought she would be living far away from these people eased her mind, as if her limbs had at last been freed from shackles.

"I'll work hard and make loads of money," she thought. She imagined everyone waiting with open arms to welcome her home.

Dark earth, clear blue rivers and streams, great expanses of forest—as the train headed north over the Musashi Plain and approached the mountains, the scenery gradually impressed on her the sadness of her journey far from home.

"Is it a town like this?" she asked Sōtarō, leaning out the window as the train came to a stop at a large station.

She saw red-faced Westerners on the platform. They appeared to be returning from Nikkō.

"Much smaller," Sōtarō replied, laughing. He seemed to be remembering with fondness the life he had led in the town and the people he knew there. "There're mountains everywhere you look. Still, it's an interesting place once you get used to it."

The train began climbing up into high country. Through breaks in the evergreen forest and over the limbs of trees swaying in the wind, Oshima could see deep gorges and distant mountain passes. The passenger car fell silent.

47

As THE MIST SWIRLING past the train-car window grew thicker, the engine slowed to a regular chugging and steadily climbed the high plateau. Misty blue-green rainbows arched from dense stands of cedar and oak. Sunlight glinted in the fine rain, and incongruous, barren-looking fields clinging low on the mountains or the random house in the shadows of thick bamboo groves caught her eye.

Before Oshima and her brother reached their destination, the train stopped at several deserted stations. The communities around them were more beautiful than the suburbs of Tokyo, but, for

Oshima, silenced, fatigued, and a little awed by the scale of the natural surroundings, they also seemed exotically strange.

"People dress like that even up here in the sticks," she mused,
staring at several of the passersby.

When they reached their station, Shiobara, it was gently raining.
They left the station, crossed a bridge, and, at what appeared to be
the edge of town, found a tea stall, a transport firm, and a few smoky
old inns. One of the shops displayed rhododendrons and a stunted
mountain pine. Oshima and her brother passed through the silent
town in two rickshas.

On the main street was a large inn, its stone gate closed, a bank,
a huge vessel to capture rainwater at its front, and a police station
equipped with a fire alarm bell.

Sōtarō's house was on a secluded, quiet backstreet. At the end of
a narrow road on which a number of houses surrounded by adobe
walls with gates fronted, Oshima noticed an expansive garden. The
woodwork of the house was delicately fashioned, and the house itself
was so recently constructed that it smelled of freshly cut timber.

Sōtarō had asked the landlord to care for the place in his
absence, and the house was occupied by the owner's young employee
and his children, playing as if the property belonged to them.

"You really think you can do business here?" Oshima muttered,
standing on the veranda after she had temporarily settled in.

"The town isn't much, but there are wealthy families in the area,"
Sōtarō replied, sitting cross-legged on the floor after he set down the
tea tray and kettle and took off his coat.

Early autumn rain was still falling. A cold, damp wind reminded
Oshima that she was in a distant land. The rumbling of a slow-turn-
ing waterwheel resounded plaintively, but Oshima could not determine the direction from which the sound came.

48

AFTER SHOWING OSHIMA the house, Sōtarō set off in the rain
for the station to supervise the delivery of the stock and luggage.
Oshima went into the kitchen to prepare dinner. Since Sōtarō lived
alone without a maid, it seemed certain that his woman made frequent visits, for the shelves and drains were clean and in good order.

Sōtarō made two trips in a cart, hauling plants from the station, and it was night by the time he had arranged them in the garden. He put on his hat and coat and left again without telling Oshima where he was going. She was so exhausted she did not awake when he returned through the back entrance early in the morning.

The next day, Oshima woke to the sound of the waterwheel. Half asleep, she lay listening to the rhythmic thumping. On realizing that today was the start of a new life in an unknown land, she remembered with fondness even those people in Tokyo she had once considered enemies.

Her brother's woman had drifted to a city two stations up the line, and, in the course of plying her trade, her contract had been bought out by a man connected with a local mine. She was now kept as his mistress in a mining town located between the city and Shiobara. Oshima had learned this before she left Tokyo. While the woman was still engaged in business in the provincial city, Sōtarō arrived, and, loafing around his inn or amusing himself at the nearby hot-spring resorts, he became acquainted with local pleasure seekers and began gambling with them. In compensation for his woman having been taken as another man's mistress, Sōtarō received a small sum of capital from the woman's new lover, and he decided to set himself up as a gardener in Shiobara, where he had established several business connections.

At about noon, as the rain lifted, Sōtarō took Oshima to meet the landlord, who lived a few hundred yards away. The landlord was the only rice miller in the town and was a wealthy man. As she passed through the gate, Oshima immediately noticed the waterwheel, which was part of a large mill. The din near the mill was so loud that she could not understand anything that anyone said, even at close range.

"All the rice produced here goes to the mine," Sōtarō informed Oshima at the entrance to the house. He paused to talk with several of the workers, who were white, covered with rice flour.

The landlord was seated at his desk in a well-lit office behind a sliding glass door. He was wearing his spectacles to read price quotations for commodities in the newspaper. But, when he caught sight of Sōtarō, he beamed and bowed politely to Oshima. His letter rack, hanging from a pillar in the room, was stuffed full of letters and telegrams, many from Tokyo. Oshima gazed in wonder at this gentleman who had adopted the style of a wealthy urban rice broker.

"This is the garden, the one I've been working on," Sōtarō explained as he guided Oshima along the stepping-stones in the garden past the man-made hill and pond. They climbed to a point where Oshima could survey a broad expanse of land, the size of a small park, with the artificial hill at its center.

"So some people really do live like this," Oshima exclaimed, looking down at the layout of the house and garden.

"He plans to fill this area with trees and turn it into a park for the people of the town. It's going to cost a small fortune, so he's waiting for the economy to improve," her brother explained.

He sat under a tree on a bench like the ones usually found around playgrounds and smoked a cigarette.

49

FROM THE FIRST, Oshima got on well with the landlord and his wife and children. She also became friendly with the people at the large inn, Hamaya, which she had seen on the main street on the day of her arrival.

Living at the inn, in addition to the young master's mother and an old man, were the master's sister, two years younger than Oshima, three maids, and the young master himself, a slender, quiet man with a white complexion and a long, thin face. This reliable-seeming young man was almost always at work in the cashier's area. He was a gentle person who never seemed to raise his voice.

As cool air came to the bleached, lonely town in the mountains, the silhouettes of peaks rising in the northwest were daily shrouded by dark gray clouds. During the depressing, rainy days, Oshima would go to the Hamaya to obtain hot water, and she often entered the house to warm herself by the fire and tell the daughter tales of Tokyo or help serve the guests who crowded the inn to capacity.

Around the dim open hearth of the inn, the plump mother of the young master and an old man, who was always busy at some task, kept the sake heated to a perfect temperature or sent the maids about their chores. A freshwater fish wholesaler who supplied the town's inns and restaurants had come from Tokyo to settle accounts and had been at the inn for several days, drinking in the recently constructed addition.

The rice miller was said to have provided the money to build this large new room, and Oshima would often go in and look around. The owner's mother seemed so proud as she pointed out the fine, straight grain of the pillars made of Japanese cypress, the sculptured woodwork around the transom windows, the broad cedar door decorated with patterns in brilliant colors, and the ornamental crosspieces of black persimmon in front of the alcove. Out of curiosity, Oshima peeked in the room to watch the performances of traditional geisha arts that the fish wholesaler was sponsoring. Dozens of geisha, the long hems of their cheap kimonos dragging on the tatami, and their apprentices, wearing secondhand crepe kimonos, their makeup crudely and spottily applied, were constantly entering and leaving the room. The cheerful rhythms of hand drums and the large drum resounded without stop. A blind male music teacher, reputed to be an expert flute player, was led past Oshima down the corridor by his geisha students.

Back by the hearth, Oshima saw the rice miller come in and take a seat by the fire. The old man dozing there rolled to his feet and withdrew from the room. Sake and a cup were placed before the rice miller, and the owner's mother emerged and served him.

"You couldn't tell by looking at them? You must be pretty naive," her brother replied to Oshima's question about the relationship between the owner's mother and the rice miller.

"The miller set her up in the business in the first place. That's why the old man closes his eyes to what's going on," her brother added.

50

THE MISTRESS SAW HER MAN off to the mine and usually came to Sōtarō before noon on Mondays, covering the three and a half miles down the mountain in a ricksha.

Her name was Okana, and her family once lived in the vicinity of the house of Oshima's natural parents. She and Sōtarō had been childhood friends. When Okana made her debut in the demimonde in Tokyo, Sōtarō had delighted in having her name tattooed on his arm. To be with this woman, Sōtarō had sent his wife home to her parents and had so disappointed his father that he had Sōtarō legally declared mentally incompetent, a form of disinheritance.

Okana, who once worked in Nihonbashi, one of Tokyo's most fashionable demimonde districts, was slender and small of stature. By the time she had exhausted her attraction for customers in Tokyo and moved to the provincial mining town, her health had been impaired and her artistic skills coarsened. She was not popular among natives of the region, but people associated with the mine made much of her.

On the days Okana arrived in the morning, she generally returned the same evening, but, when her patron was away in Tokyo on business, she would stay with Sōtarō for several nights. At times, she called him to her side at a hot-spring resort located five miles up in the mountains.

Okana arrived at a languid pace, dressed in the fashion of respectable women, not having bothered to put makeup on her mountain-weathered face. She never failed to bring Oshima a gift such as hard jelly cake, which was a specialty of the region.

While the woman was present, Oshima left to visit the rice miller or the Hamaya.

The rice miller's wife was a woman with good taste who spoke and dressed in the manner of sophisticated Tokyo wives. She stayed at home and cared for her husband's son, born to the widow of the Hamaya, and her own two natural daughters.

Oshima was playing with neighborhood children in the miller's park. "Shall we go see your aunt at Hamaya?" she asked, gazing at the miller's handsome son.

"All right," he replied nodding his head.

"Who do you like best, your mother or your aunt?" she asked, trying to discover how much the boy knew, but he appeared not to understand.

Oshima sat down on the bench. Time was dragging by. The leaves of cherry trees planted around the playground were turning yellow or had fallen from their branches, and distant autumn-like clouds were moving across the sky. She thought of the young owner of the Hamaya, who occasionally sat opposite her at the hearth of his inn. His wife, who had come from a provincial city, had been sent back to her parents to recover from lung disease and had not lived with her husband for some time.

51

THE FIELD OF GARDEN PLANTS and the flower beds that Oshima took such pleasure in caring for were now covered with frost. As mountain winds blew down, assaulting the town, whistling through eaves and cracks, plastering the sides of houses with leaves and debris, Sōtarō, with no work to occupy himself, spent more and more time away gambling with his friends.

Of the plants Sōtarō had brought with him, many were unsuited to the mountain soil and had withered before they could be sold, this despite Oshima's diligent efforts to save them. Sōtarō's expectations for the flower seeds were utterly dashed. Not only did they not sell as well as he had hoped, but, after they were planted, many did not germinate, and the growth of others was impaired. Disheartened by the failure of his business, Sōtarō seemed to find the idea of spending the winter holed up in the isolated town with Oshima intolerable.

Snow came to the mountains. Most mornings, packhorses carrying miso, soy, and other supplies to the mine stood in line, their tails limp in the early winter rain, their white breath filling the street. On rare sunny days, Oshima went for her customary walk along the tree-lined road to the sawmill, but lately the loggers and workers had all disappeared, and the mill stood quiet and deserted. The pleasure quarter, its two- and three-story buildings painted white, was located in the midst of rice paddies across a small river from the sawmill. The trees around it were bare.

But customers continued to frequent the Hamaya to drink, though Oshima did not know where they came from. The Hamaya was the only establishment in town that called geisha this late in the season. Oshima occasionally saw them as they passed, the hems of their skirts held high, accompanied by their male attendants. The thought occurred to her to ask for work at the eating and drinking places or one of the local inns she saw on the street. These establishments, it was said, kept cheap prostitutes during the off-season. But on considering the kinds of customers she would have to serve—local farmers or small-time silk-cocoon buyers—she was repulsed by the idea.

When Sōtarō returned penniless from his gambling, he often took Oshima's clothes and other possessions to pawn at the shop of one of his acquaintances, but, once this source of money was exhausted, he had no other choice but to cajole or beg money from his woman, Okana.

From time to time, Oshima was sent to collect the promised sums. She trudged alone along the mountain road over one pass after another. On the outskirts of the mining town, there were extensive tracts of housing as well as tea stalls and bars. The woman was being kept in a district of blacksmiths displaying horseshoes and agricultural tools.

"It's a wonder Okana puts up with this place," Oshima thought, but Okana's small house looked elegant and tidy. Inside, Oshima found it comfortably furnished, with Tokyo-style chests and a large brazier.

52

AFTER OSHIMA HAD PAID OKANA a few visits, though, it became clear that Okana was not living as comfortably as Sōtarō had thought. According to Okana, her patron was in charge of extending rails in the mine. He went down into the mine with the ordinary miners. The monthly allowance he provided her for living expenses and spending money amounted to very little. Her patron had heard rumors about her relationship with Sōtarō from people associated with the mine, and now he was even more reluctant to give her money. This was the cause of frequent quarrels. In the summer, Okana visited a hot-spring resort deep in the mountains for her health, and she was commuting to see a doctor in the nearby provincial city. With the cooler weather, she had begun to regain weight, but her color was still poor. For Okana, accustomed to lively urban settings, the cruelest blow was to be forced to spend the long, hard winter in this isolated town surrounded by mountains. It was as if she had entered a deep, dark hole. How she longed to take up her former trade in a warmer land! Okana often talked this plan over with Sōtarō.

At about the time Okana had received a final cash settlement from her patron and left, with only the clothes she was wearing, for Chiba prefecture, where she hoped to get back in the business with the help of a friend, Sōtarō's economic situation was desperate. The month was December, and the mountains were pure white. Day after day, the town was pelted either by sleet or by snow, and the snow level inched higher.

Depressed by the lack of response to his letters to his father pleading for money, Sōtarō left Shiobara in the latter part of December. Okana sent him traveling expenses. Oshima, who was to stay behind, saw her brother off at the nearby station, which, except for them, was deserted. It was decided that Oshima would remain under the supervision of the miller and Hamaya's widow as security for the unpaid rent and small sums Sōtarō had borrowed in Shiobara.

Lacking warm clothing to protect him from the cold winter air, Sōtarō, an ancient umbrella in hand and dressed like a fugitive at large, boarded the train. Only his sunken eyes, gleaming wildly, were visible beneath the brim of his tweed cap.

It had been snowing off and on since evening. Without the means to prepare even one garment with cotton padding for winter, Oshima, wearing a thin summer kimono, left the empty station after the train had departed. She seemed a lonely figure as she walked away, shivering in the cold, carrying a coarse oil-paper umbrella inscribed with the name *Hamaya* in large characters.

"My brother's played me for a complete fool!" she said to herself, finally aware of how far she had fallen in the world.

From the cheap restaurants and bars where prostitutes plied their trade, the steam of boiling food wafted out, dimly white on the cold wind.

53

TRAVEL TO THE TOWN almost ceased until May or June, when the silk-cocoon buyers and itinerant merchants began appearing on the second-floor verandas of cheap inns. The Hamaya, designated as the temporary quarters of prefectural officials, was the only inn in town that still put up the occasional guest, usually men dressed in Western-style clothing. Among them were railroad bureaucrats and insurance agents, but, by January, even these sorts of visitors stopped coming. The people at the Hamaya suffered through the long, tedious hours huddled around the open hearth.

Finished with the morning's dusting and sweeping, Oshima joined the others around the fire. Gossip made the time pass quickly, but, when the owner's mother, who was addicted to cards and had played deep into the previous night, emerged from her bedroom, Oshima left the warmth of the hearth.

"Can't waste the rest of the day," she declared.

Since some of the female help had been let go for the winter, Oshima was kept busy working in the kitchen, and, when the owner's mother saw that Oshima had a free moment, she assigned her another task. This generally involved washing the sleeping robes, pillows, and bedding the guests would use in the spring. Oshima did much of this tedious work in a large banquet room upstairs, where she took the articles apart and sewed them back together after they were washed. When she began to feel depressed, she would hum songs to herself as she mechanically did her sewing, but, on occasion, she was assaulted by an intense loneliness.

Opening the window, she saw the distant white peaks outlined against the dark gray sky, and she imagined the lives of the workers laboring in the mine deep in the mountains. She heard the sporadic chirping of birds in a large cage on the veranda of the room below.

In the evening, when the electric lights dimly illuminated the inn, the rest of the town was closed up tight. The mill's waterwheel echoed dully across the snow-covered fields and gardens in back of the inn. Oshima, who worked so briskly, always careful to show others a cheerful attitude, was often overcome by sadness when by herself.

The miller usually arrived as everyone gathered around the open hearth in the evening and then went to soak his large body in the hot bath. When Oshima's turn came to bathe, the miller had finished his nightly drink and was stretched out cozily in his bed, but the owner's mother and regulars from the town continued slapping cards down in his quiet room late into the night.

Oshima sometimes found herself alone at the open hearth with the inn's young owner. He did not drink and had no interest in playing cards. Oshima had recently been assigned the task of looking after the personal needs of this young man, who seemed preoccupied and worried about his wife, still living with her parents, unable to decide whether she was cured.

54

ONE MORNING, as she always did, Oshima was sweeping out the young man's room, located off the interior garden across from the new addition. Two new chests of clothing, locked as they were when the bride brought them, occupied a corner of the dark room. As Oshima gingerly swept around the chests, the anxiety and regret returned. She worked more quickly, fearful that she would betray her sense of guilt if spoken to or observed. After breakfast with the owner's sisters, Oshima hurried off to the bathroom to be alone with her thoughts. Mist from the previous night's bath lightly covered the surface of a full-length mirror hanging beneath the stained-glass window. Oshima viewed her distorted image in the mirror. She pitied her reflected body, abandoned to work in this distant place, so far from family and friends.

She stepped down to the concrete floor to let the water out of the bath. Her eyes filled with tears, blurring the swirl of draining water. Raised among strangers, she had been trained from an early age to make those around her as comfortable as possible. She remembered how she had washed the young innkeeper's back the night before. It depressed her that she lacked the will to reject the young man's unexpected advances.

"I've had it with men like Tsuru," she had thought, unsure of herself, as though she were drowning.

Grasping the edge of the tub, she gazed transfixed as the last of the water gurgled down the drain.

Through the glass door, she caught a glimpse of the thin, elegantly dressed innkeeper as he crossed the bridge on his way to his warehouses in back. It was the first time she had seen him that morning. The night before, the sensation of touching his delicate arms and legs and the white skin of his body was strangely unpleasant, but now she felt these same features held a certain attraction.

"There's mail for you," the young man said, entering the bathroom and producing a letter for Oshima.

It was from her father in Ōji.

"What can it be?" she declared, drying her hands with a towel before taking the letter. She opened the envelope and examined its contents.

55

OSHIMA HAD RECEIVED several more letters from her father by the time the snow had melted from the mountains, revealing bare peaks rising in relief against the blue sky.

Spring winds refreshed the closed air of the inn's old rooms, and, for a number of days, the town shimmered in the heat. Light snow flurries visited the region, but the snow melted almost as soon as it touched the ground. Sunlight formed a series of beautiful rainbows playing on mists spraying from slight cracks in storage tubs. The hum of kite strings filled the air, and a candy man in the street in front of the inn called children by beating on his large drum.

"Warmer weather, isn't it?" was the standard greeting heard around the open hearth at the Hamaya.

In the garden at the back of the inn, a soft breeze caressed Oshima's neck. Scattered plum trees were on the verge of bursting into flower. Oshima recalled with longing the sky over Tokyo.

"I've received another letter from my father," Oshima told her young man, showing him the letter when they were alone.

The man had stopped his customary visits to his wife before the New Year. His sisters observed their brother and Oshima whispering together at the entrance to the bath or in front of the room upstairs.

Her father's letters invariably ordered Oshima to stop wasting her time in the provinces and return home. Oshima could tell from the tone of the letters that her old-fashioned father was disturbed by rumors about her present condition.

"What shall I do?" Oshima exclaimed with a sigh. Tears formed in her eyes. But the couple's conversations always ended inconclusively, without determining whether she should return.

"Father thinks I've become a whore," she said, laughing.

They talked of running away to Tokyo together, but the Hamaya's owner, who had never worked anywhere else, was not foolhardy enough to choose such an extreme course of action. He spoke of setting Oshima up in her own house in the nearby provincial city. But Oshima knew that this was not possible because he would have to justify the expense to the miller, who had done so much to help the inn prosper.

At about the beginning of May, engineers and construction workers, who were building a dam meant to generate electric power in a gorge three and a half miles away, started to gather at the inn from Tokyo and the surrounding mountains. By that time, people had ceased to remark on the relationship between the young man and Oshima.

56

THE MOTHER OF THE MASTER of the Hamaya arranged for Oshima to go into service at a hot-spring resort owned by a distant relative. She was afraid that rumors of her son's affair might reach his wife's parents and also afraid of what the neighbors were thinking. Oshima left at the end of May.

Following the small river at the edge of Shiobara, and winding her way up the road through the mountains, after a considerable climb, Oshima suddenly encountered the white walls and heavy beamed roofs of the hot-spring resort. Fourteen inns packed tightly together on both sides of the steep, rocky road constituted the resort area. The road narrowed, and the small river had become a fast-running mountain stream, chattering ceaselessly.

Oshima was sent to one of the oldest houses in the area. To accommodate people in the region who came to celebrate when the silkworms began spinning or on other such occasions, a new second story had recently been constructed, its back flush against the side of a cliff. The new addition was larger than the ground floor, originally constructed as a warehouse with a cellar. The garden was alive with the leaves of columbine and the pink damask flowers of mountain roses, their colors melting into the sunlight.

On opening the second-floor shutters, closed tight during the deep snows of winter, Oshima saw green barley growing in fields newly cultivated up the steep sides of the mountains. Small birds were singing happily on the tiled roofs of warehouses. Morning clouds, strangely beautiful through the branches of mountain pines, reminded her how deep she had traveled into the mountains.

The cocoon harvest had not yet started, so Oshima rarely saw local farmers or merchants living near the resort area. She was again set to work sewing. One day she met an art student, who came dashing in with his box of paints.

"What're you doing in these mountains?" Oshima asked. His Tokyo dialect, which she had not heard for so long, filled her with nostalgia, and she found an opportunity to speak with the young man.

The student, in casual dress, with the lunch that Oshima had prepared for him, set off nonchalantly. He would cross the mountain pass before the sunrise's reddish-tinged clouds dissipated over the peaks.

"What a carefree student! Such a handsome young man!" Oshima, as if envious, remarked to her mistress as they watched the young man stride up the mountain road.

The household consisted of the owner, a woman in her thirties, and her seven-year-old adopted daughter, and, since there were no old people, Oshima found the resort a relatively pleasant place to work. On sunny days, the pale, ill owner would sometimes sew upstairs in a room with good exposure, but, in general, she confined herself to her own dim room.

The summer sun beat down on the impoverished village wedged among the mountains. Oshima heard a tree frog chirping on the trunk of the persimmon tree in the garden, and then huge drops of rain, like bits of silver, suddenly pelted the young green leaves. At about three in the afternoon, she had been overcome by drowsiness, but now her mind was clear and awake. Leaning on the bannister of the upstairs veranda, Oshima gazed out at the beautiful sheets of summer rain. Her subdued heart sprang to life.

57

THE MASTER of the Hamaya came to see her twice.

The first time, he bathed in the hot spring and spent the night. Two days later he visited her again. This time he brought Oshima's father, who had arrived unexpectedly at his inn. Oshima, bearing the little girl on her back, was wandering up a mountain path through fields, picking wildflowers along the way. Even in this village there was a poorer outskirts, and several small, dirty houses were perched on the slope above her. In the mornings and evenings, the temperatures were about what they were in Tokyo in April, but, by noon, the strong sun of midsummer seemed to penetrate her skin and eyes, and the smell of steaming vegetation arose all around her. With each rain, the young mulberry leaves gleamed a dark green.

The Hamaya's owner found her crouched by an irrigation ditch in the shade of a farmer's wisteria arbor. She was showing the girl red carp.

"Your father's arrived from Tokyo," he whispered as he drew next to her.

"My father's here!" Oshima exclaimed in a breathless shout. "What time did he arrive?" she asked, staring at the innkeeper.

"Probably about eleven o'clock. As soon as he met me, he started insisting on taking you home. I told him you were up here, and he said he'd go alone to fetch you, so what could I do?"

She listened without wiping away the perspiration rolling down her cheeks. "He's an impatient man," she concluded with a sigh. "What's he doing now?"

"He's waiting for you down at the resort. It looks like he's going to drag you back as soon as he sets his eyes on you!"

Oshima turned pale, and her voice trembled. "I can't meet my father here," she said, clenching her hands into a tight ball. "Don't you have a scheme to get rid of him?"

"But I've already told him you're here."

"That was a mistake."

"I think you ought to meet him at least. Then we can convince him."

Oshima, her head cocked to the side, was lost in thought, and her expression turned ferocious. "When I left Tokyo, I made a solemn vow to my parents that I'd never be a burden on them again. It's torture to meet him here like this," she muttered.

Tears were streaming down her face.

"I suppose there's no way around it. I'll have to talk to him," she said after a long silence. "If we reason with him, maybe we can work something out."

They left the shade of the wisteria arbor and proceeded down the path.

58

HER FATHER WAS SEATED sternly at the entrance amid the clutter of scales and a grandfather clock. He was smoking tobacco from the pouch Oshima remembered from her childhood. A great deal of coaxing was needed before Oshima and the owner of the Hamaya could persuade her father to enter the house and sit in the room used for receiving guests.

"Thank you for coming," she said, overcome with emotion, but she could not remain seated next to her father, who appeared about to speak, and, with this meaningless greeting, she began bustling about, preparing tea and bringing out small cakes.

"There's really no need to worry about me. But, since you've come all this way, you should enjoy yourself and bathe in the hot spring."

"No time! This is a one-day trip," he snapped. His face was strained as he once again pulled out his pipe. "I don't know what kind of mess you're involved in here, but you're coming home with me today," he continued.

"I'm not in any sort of trouble," Oshima said, laughing. From her father's words and his first letter, she knew that her family thought her brother had sold her into prostitution.

Her father insisted that he would talk with the holder of her contract, pay off her debt, and take her back to Tokyo. Oshima tried to avoid discussing the problem and played for time by serving her father sake and then dinner. At last, she found an opportunity to slip into the back room to consult with the innkeeper. Night fell on their whispered conversation, as the young man could not decide what to do.

"Even in death I won't become your mistress! My father's so old-fashioned, he'd be furious at the mere suggestion." Oshima refused the owner's offer to talk with her father about setting her up in her own house. His final proposal was to obtain money in secret from the miller and buy her a business in the nearby provincial city. She knew that the owner had to be thinking of his wife, whose health had been improving since the spring, when she started taking a new medicine from Tokyo. It had been agreed that his wife would return to him soon. His concern for the woman only deepened Oshima's affection for him. Their conversation in the small room continued late into the rainy night.

By morning, the rain had lifted, and the weather was fine. When Oshima got up, she discovered her father smoking, neatly dressed and waiting as if he expected to leave immediately.

59

HER EYES SWOLLEN and puffy, Oshima served her father breakfast. A cool morning breeze blew through the room from the open sliding doors, and frogs croaked merrily in the rice fields.

"It's going to rain. We won't be able to return to Tokyo today," she murmured as she stood on the veranda and watched the dark, heavy clouds approaching.

"I really don't know how things stand. Maybe they don't want money at all," Oshima replied, feigning innocence when her father produced fifty large gold coins from his money belt and declared that this ought to be enough to settle her debt.

"Let's compromise, Father. This family's been good to me, and it looks like the inn will become busy soon. If I leave now, I'll be acting in bad faith, so let me stay for all of June. I'll be back in Tokyo by the Festival of Souls at the latest," Oshima offered, trying to pacify her father and persuade him to go home alone. But the old man would not listen. No good would come of her hanging around a place like this, he insisted. There were rumors around the neighborhood about his daughter drifting through the provinces.

"But I can't leave today. I'll have to stop by the Hamaya, and I can't go without saying good-bye at the miller's. And my hair, I'll have to get my hair done," she exclaimed in exasperation, and she stormed out of the room. The father at last showed the temper he was known for as a young tradesman and fumed about local hoodlums wrapping their tentacles around his daughter's body.

"You and I can't settle this. Bring me the person in charge!" he shouted in a shrill voice.

Ill at ease alone in the corridor, Oshima left for the bath. Through the glass door, she made out the pale face of her lover rising in the steam from the large wooden tub.

Poking her head inside, Oshima declared with a sigh, "The stubborn old man won't listen to a word I say." They continued to discuss what she should do but again arrived at no conclusion.

By the time the young owner had gotten dressed, Oshima had vanished from the house.

Oshima was stumbling up into the mountains by herself. Young vegetation was so luxuriant it seemed to suffocate her. She saw fields of blooming rapeseed, and light smoke wafted up into the sky from a pottery kiln in the shadow of a peak streaked with red. Oshima gained control of herself and strode briskly up the quiet mountain path. She wanted to be alone, to find a place where she could weep to her heart's content.

60

RELYING ON DIRECTIONS from a person who saw Oshima climbing deep in the mountains, her father and the innkeeper discovered her crouched like a hunted rabbit in a grassy field by the edge of a gorge.

Below the cliff that was dotted with the red flowers of mountain azalea, rapids rushed against random boulders and sent up a cool mist. A precarious log bridged the two banks of the gorge. Tempted by a perverse desire to find a place where she might imagine her own death, she descended to the edge of the gorge, but the sound of the river and the quiet of her surroundings had calmed her agitated mind.

Hearing human voices, Oshima leaped to her feet and saw two men crashing down the slope, parting pine branches as they came. She stiffened with embarrassment.

Her father supporting one arm and the young man the other, she was guided down the narrow mountain path. At times, the ground in front of her blurred through her tears.

Forced into a ricksha by her father, she left the resort town at ten in the morning. As she descended to Shiobara, the sound of rushing water that had occupied her mind for so many months gradually gave way to the ringing of wheels on the rocky road.

She crossed a dry riverbed showing the ravages of summer floods, and the town of Shiobara appeared before her. A blacksmith's shop and a cooper in one impoverished neighborhood triggered pleasant memories of the town. In front of the houses she passed, there were huge piles of white silk cocoons. Cocoon buyers, who gathered at the height of summer from all parts of the country, lent the crowded town a lively, prosperous air.

Oshima served her father at the Hamaya and exchanged only a few words with her lover before her father hustled her off to the station. Out of sight, the young man followed on backstreets.

"If you're ever in trouble and have no place to go, don't hesitate to come back here," he whispered, taking Oshima aside to give her the train ticket he had purchased for her.

Silk-cocoon buyers with their briefcases and large parcels crowded the station. On the train, the talk was all of cocoons and the raw silk market. She stuck her head out the window of the car to see the young man, wearing his tweed hunting cap, disappear down a backstreet. The sight remained in her mind for a long time. But, once the train was on its way, she had fewer and fewer thoughts of Shiobara and the resort town deep in the mountains. Deep stands of cedar and dark forests stretched before her eyes. Shadows from young leaves waving in the breeze flickered across her face.

She thought of her mother, probably waiting in delight for the perfect victim to torture. Oshima began considering places she might stay to avoid her.

61

As the train descended to the Musashi plain, the humid air, gently sloping fields and rice paddies, and lowland forests of small trees made Oshima feel like a fish returned to water. Yet, with each passing station, the closer to Tokyo they drew, she grew more distressed from a sense of impending crisis.

"I won't go to either my mother's or my sister's," she thought. "I don't want to see anyone I knew before, not Tsuru or Uegen, until I've made some kind of life for myself."

They arrived at Ōji station toward evening. In a dark mood, Oshima followed her father as if he were dragging her. Lights were on in her family's quiet neighborhood. All seemed domestic and familiar after the wild nature of the mountains.

Her father entered first, carrying a rhododendron with its roots wrapped in newspaper, a plant that he had found in the mountains, and a present of sweet jelly, a specialty of the Shiobara region. Oshima's sister was sitting with her mother in the room off the kitchen. They both seemed to be waiting for Oshima's return. Oshima saw that her sister's three-year-old son was walking.

"They grow up so fast!" she declared after a few brusque greetings. She scooped up the child and put him on her lap, as if she had found a balm for her wounded pride.

"Don't you remember your aunt? I was always spoiling you." The child, a piece of jelly candy in his hand, immediately took to Oshima.

"My, how dark you've become!" her sister remarked, gazing with amusement at Oshima's mountain-tanned face. Oshima's countrified appearance caused even her dull sister to imagine the sort of place she had been living.

"Everybody looks down on the provinces, but it was a wonderful place," Oshima declared with conviction.

"What's there to do up in the mountains?" her sister responded.

"I felt the same at first, but, after I lived there, I realized how wrong I was! You have the hot springs, and the town's so beautiful. People are kind, and there're restaurants you'll never find in Ōji and geisha houses, too. I'd love to take you there and show you."

"Oshima's found a boyfriend. That's why she likes the place," her sister teased.

"Liar!" Oshima snorted. "I know what you were saying behind my back. You thought I'd become a whore. But actually people trusted me there. There's an investor who said he'd help me start my own business if I stayed."

"Hooked yourself a rich patron, huh?" her sister countered.

62

FLOATING IN HER DREAMS of the mountains, Oshima was soon shocked back to reality by the taunts of her cruel mother. "Stubborn bitch!" "Good-for-nothing slut!"—insults that she had grown used to before leaving for the mountains now reopened festering wounds in her heart.

After the Festival of Souls that summer, Oshima was sent to Tokyo's Shitaya ward to live with her aunt, her father's cousin. The aunt was the beloved wife of a famous samurai swordsman, who, when the age changed, had obtained a position as a coachman with the Imperial Household Agency but had been dismissed because of alcoholism and had died shortly thereafter. The widowed aunt never remarried and raised her daughter on her own by teaching the samisen to girls in the neighborhood. Now she survived on money sent by her daughter, who was in business, and by taking in piecework.

As the sake that she occasionally drank began to circulate through her withered veins, the old woman recounted stories from the past. She would take down her samisen from the wall and, plucking it with her fingers, intone popular songs from the Edo period. A sooty portrait of her husband, the famous swordsman, was mounted on a wall beam.

Oshima visited this aunt several times after she left her foster family, but the woman's continued concern with her personal appearance despite her age irritated the roughly raised Oshima. The formal portrait of her husband in court dress with his pale, beautiful features and sharply defined forehead, eyebrows, and mustache seemed incongruous to Oshima in the small, dusty house.

"Was your husband really such a handsome gentleman?" she asked, laughing as she gazed in wonder at the photograph.

The swordsman, in his youth, was the retainer of a certain lord, and, because of this connection, he witnessed the famous Sakurada Gate Incident. The old woman described in detail how, on that snowy evening in 1860, eighteen masterless samurai cut down Ii Naosuke, the shogun's great councillor, for his signing of a treaty of commerce with the foreign barbarians. On another occasion, the aunt and her husband had taken their daughter to Asakusa, and the child accidentally bumped against a sweet sake merchant carrying his goods balanced on a pole on his shoulder. The man attacked the child, wielding his pole like a sword. The aunt's husband picked him up, threw him down to the ground, and shamed him in front of the gathering crowd. For Oshima, such stories conjured up only dramatic scenes from the stage.

"My aunt can't forget her husband." The longer Oshima lived with the old woman, the more she sympathized with her.

"A woman always remembers the youth she sacrificed for her man," she also thought.

Her aunt did not sew clothing of high quality but was nevertheless surrounded by a ceaseless flow of work, some of it the gaudy costumes of geisha.

When the aunt observed Oshima becoming careless with her sewing, she would rap her knuckles with a ruler.

Oshima was most useful for simple jobs that had to be done quickly.

63

IN THE MIDST of the start of a war with a foreign country, a war producing varied, new employment for many busy people, Oshima resolved for the first time to devote herself to work in which she could invest all her purpose of mind and physical strength. She did so in partnership with a tailor named Onoda, a young man who occasionally brought customers' orders for simple garments of serge or flannel to Oshima's aunt, with whom he was on friendly terms. From time to time, Onoda would come over to the side of Oshima's cutting board and stretch out to chat and joke.

At about the time the young owner of the Hamaya returned to his mountain home after a brief visit to Tokyo, Oshima had come to realize that, until then, she had been forced to survive by blind reaction or submission to authority, a way of life that left her close to slavery. How she longed to work solely for herself for once!

The innkeeper had received occasional postcards from Oshima since her return to Tokyo, and one day, when chrysanthemums were in bloom, he had shown up at the door without notice, asking for Oshima. During his three-day stay, Oshima took him to Asakusa, the theater, and vaudeville shows and visited him in his lodgings close to Ueno station.

He was no longer content to sit in the cashier's area of his inn and had begun speculating in mining properties. He spent a great deal of time traveling to investigate possible investments. His trip to Tokyo had to do with these business affairs.

"Be patient. When one of my real estate deals pays off, I'll take care of you." Apparently, the young man was still intent on keeping her by setting her up in a business in the demimonde of a provincial city.

"Do you really think I'm going to live in those mountains again?" she laughed. "I won't be your mistress!" she declared in parting.

He had given her a small sum of money, and, when she saw him off at the station, he promised to return to Tokyo in the winter. Exhausted from the profligacy of the previous days, Oshima left the station disoriented, comparing in her tired mind the innkeeper and the young tailor.

64

ONODA BROUGHT IN a bundle of garments intended for troops on the battlefront overseas, now faced with the onset of frigid weather. "How'd you like to give me a hand with this job?" he asked Oshima.

Onoda was employed at a workshop manufacturing ready-made clothing, but, when new orders flooded in owing to the outbreak of war, they proved too much for his fellow workers, and he began taking work out of his company, which held the contract, for the final stages of production. He was now busy making the rounds of people who might subcontract some of the work from him.

"You can have as much to do as you want. I can't keep up with it now as it is," Onoda declared as he brought in a load of what he called "blankets" on his back. He then began teaching Oshima what tasks she had to perform on the order that she had agreed to try her hand at.

What Onoda referred to as "blankets" were overcoats to protect against the cold—reddish-brown garments that the soldiers put on over their heads. Oshima soon accustomed her quick fingers to sewing on the buttons and hooks and darning the buttonholes of the blankets, which were already assembled to a stage at which they could be worked on by a woman without a sewing machine.

"Each of these you finish is worth thirteen sen," Onoda told her. In one day, Oshima completed fourteen or fifteen overcoats, four or five times the quantity of work done by the average woman.

The busy Onoda arrived to collect what Oshima had finished, but he was soon nodding off by her side as she kept up her rapid pace of sewing.

Oshima had little trouble making about two yen a day, and the purse tucked in her obi was always filled and rustling with the money that seemed to spin from her fingers.

"No worries about spending money if I take this woman as my lover." Onoda had awoken from his nap and sat watching Oshima as she busily darned a buttonhole. He was amazed at the intensity with which she labored.

"Make me your lover, you'll find out," Oshima declared with a smile.

"Fine with me!" Onoda said as he gathered up the finished garments. He took these back with him on his bicycle.

As Oshima grew used to sewing on hooks or darning buttonholes, these tasks became unbearably tedious.

Toward the end of the year, she learned how to operate the sewing machine at the workshop where Onoda was employed, the place that held the contract for Onoda's piecework. She was soon able to sew quite proficiently, even difficult officers' uniforms on the machine.

"What are all these frills for? Men are such sissies," Oshima exclaimed, making the slow bunch on the factory floor laugh.

It often happened that, on hauling the finished products to the government office at Tameike, which was functioning as a temporary depot for the Bureau of Clothing, ill-tempered officials there criticized the workmanship and were reluctant to accept the garments.

"If you won't take these, what will you accept?" Oshima declared when she went in place of the men to deliver the clothing. The fast-talking Oshima easily won over the bureaucrat, who at first pushed the garments away, complaining that the sewing machine had missed stitches or that the quality of the cloth was inferior.

65

Oshima gradually realized that she was more interested in using her mind to make the rounds of customers and obtain orders than in sitting all day in front of a factory sewing machine producing clothing worth a yen or two. She embraced the ambition to establish her own shop tailoring Western-style clothing.

"We've handled a great many garments, but I've never dealt with a woman tailor," said several of the officials at the Bureau of Clothing, whose friendship Oshima soon won during her frequent visits to deliver clothing. Their praise for her brisk, efficient manner of doing business convinced Oshima that she had the talent to succeed.

"I don't see why a woman can't be a tailor," she mentioned to Onoda on one of his frequent calls during slack periods at the factory.

Onoda had seen what a hard worker Oshima was, and her resolve to learn the trade matched his scheme to make her his woman and put her to work.

"Why not?" he muttered, smiling broadly. Oshima could not decide whether this taciturn man was stupid or experienced in the ways of the world. He had been indentured as an apprentice at the age of twenty in Nagoya and was now thirty. His wide, prominent nose and high cheeks gave his face a comical aspect, but he was tall and had beautiful hair, and, when he dressed in a suit, his sternly dignified, well-built figure somehow made Oshima feel secure.

At times, she spoke without reserve to the stolid, silent Onoda: "You're the homeliest man I've ever met!"

Onoda merely laughed in reply.

"But at least you don't look like a tailor. Don't government officials dress like that?"

Having found something wanting in the soft, pliant Tsuru, always dressed in his shopkeeper's apron, and the innkeeper, who was merely beautiful, as delicately featured as a waxwork doll, Oshima was attracted to Onoda's imposing bearing.

"I'm going to take Onoda out of that workshop and make him a man with my very own hands," she resolved.

As she grew more familiar with the inarticulate, sleepy-looking Onoda, she came to embrace an extraordinary affection and ambition for him.

"Tailoring's not a bad trade, but you need a lot of capital. You've got to stock expensive foreign fabrics, so your money's always asleep," he told Oshima.

"With capital, you can succeed in any business. How much would it cost to start a little shop?" she asked.

"Depends on the shop. For a place facing the main street in a commercial district, you'd need quite a sum."

66

BY THE TIME OSHIMA and Onoda found a suitable small house in the Shiba ward and started their business, it was almost December.

Oshima made several visits to her family seeking capital for the venture. On hearing success stories of small shops that had grown into large enterprises, Oshima was impatient to begin work. Passing profitable shops, big or small, made her arms tingle. Of the small businesses that she understood were making money, those selling Western-style goods most appealed to her nature.

"I've seen a place in the Tamachi district," Oshima reported to Onoda soon after her return. The rental house was formerly a neighborhood post office. It measured about twelve feet by eighteen feet. She thought that, if they spent some money for a few repairs, it would function well enough.

"It's just right for a new business," she added.

The landlord was the owner of the neighboring sake shop.

"We can turn it into a workable shop for less than a hundred yen. The rent's cheap, and we can borrow the landlord's phone," Onoda concluded after he had seen the property.

No matter how many times Oshima entreated her family, her mother adamantly refused to provide her with capital, but she was finally able to cart off the clothes and furniture that she had collected during her marriage to Tsuru. She and Onoda sold the clothing.

Oshima remembered that Oyū's father had once hired a journeyman carpenter in the Atago district of Shiba ward, and, after he agreed to do the work, the former post office was transformed into a shop: the earthen floor was boarded over, the ceiling papered, and cheap, used tatami, thirty sen a piece, hauled in.

Oshima and Onoda moved on a rainy day. Wood scraps and shavings still covered the damp earthen floor. Shelving cost more than expected, and, before the room began to resemble a real tailor's shop, Oshima was forced to empty her purse a number of times. After the carpenter went home, leaving his toolbox in the corner, Oshima once again opened her chests and removed another garment. She quietly slipped out the rear entrance.

The streets were taking on the celebratory air of the year's end. Oshima boarded a crowded streetcar and rode through the busy city, boasting of its prosperity with red flags and crimson lanterns. Oshima's thoughts hurried on ahead to the pawnshop close to her aunt's house.

67

ONCE THE SEWING MACHINE and cutting board were in place—Oshima did not have enough to pay for these outright but was able to convince the salesmen to leave them on credit—and they had hired two transient workmen and a young apprentice, they began working on a subcontract that Onoda had received from the Bureau of Clothing.

"We have mountains of work, and there's enough profit to make it interesting. I promise we'll return the garments by the end of the year," Oshima assured one of her aunt's customers, a woman with a large wardrobe. Onoda sent Oshima to borrow the clothing and pawn it for payment toward the sewing machine and the cutting board, but, on the way home with her precariously obtained capital, she spent most of it on impulse for a grandfather clock and a hanging scroll.

"They're for the shop. It's a capital investment for the business," she responded when scolded by Onoda. But Onoda, too, seemed impressed by his first business and gazed around the shop in wonder.

"Keep working! When the money rolls in, we won't forget you!" Oshima called out to the sleepy-looking workmen. She felt a boundless joy and pride in the thought that her will alone kept the sewing machine humming and the irons banging late into the night.

In the midst of the frantic activity, Oshima occasionally noticed the disheveled Onoda, who, even in the morning, seemed slightly exhausted.

"There he goes again," she muttered, putting down her sewing needle to study Onoda, dozing off at his seat in front of the cutting board. "I've never heard of the illness he's got!"

The workmen snickered.

"How'd he complete the term of his apprenticeship with work like that?" she added.

"Shut up!" Onoda blustered, regaining consciousness and resuming the task at hand.

The deadline for payments of debt, the last day of December, came with Oshima and Onoda owing money to a number of people. There was the rent, which they had borrowed from an acquaintance, the monthly payment for the sewing machine, and the interest due at the pawnshop. She also had to worry about the carpenter's wages, which she had not fully paid.

"At this rate, we'll never catch up," Oshima concluded, calculating in her mind the sums they would receive by the end of the year. Seated in front of the brazier, her arms folded, she gravely considered their situation.

"We'll have to earn far greater profits," she concluded.

68

THEY FORCED THEIR ACHING limbs on until two or three in the morning for several days at a stretch and kept working up to the final minutes before the dawn of the first day of the New Year.

As night deepened, the sporadic cacophony from a band of clarinets and samisen advertising products on the main commercial street drifted in, sounding vaguely dispirited. The dry rustling of bamboo grass attached to the entrance as a New Year's decoration irritated Oshima, whose nerves were frayed. Street sounds, receding and advancing as the wind changed, reminded her of the tide.

The hoarse conversations of the workmen ceased, and, from time to time, Oshima's mind, heavy from lack of sleep, was swept by waves of dizziness. Loud banging as the iron hit the cutting table rang in her ears. The sewing machine started up and revolved with a maddening racket.

"He's finally fallen asleep," said one of the workmen.

Onoda, who had been sipping sake to ward off the cold, was slumbering curled up on the floor.

"Doesn't he know the date?" Oshima exclaimed.

"We all admire the way you never seem to need rest," the workman continued.

"I can go for days without sleep and feel fine," Oshima replied cheerfully.

While it was still dark, Oshima and the apprentice threw bundles of the newly manufactured clothing over their shoulders and hurried off to the Bureau of Clothing to receive payment. After paying the landlord, several small debts to shops, and part of the wages owed the workmen, Oshima and Onoda had almost nothing left.

"As you see, we're in a terrible mess," Oshima said at the entrance, attempting to get rid of the woman from whom she had borrowed the garments she had pawned, and she went inside without a glance at the woman.

The shop was in chaos. Work was scattered throughout the room. Flattened rice cakes lay in the corner, and wreaths and other decorations for the New Year were piled on top of them.

"You're one of the people we simply can't pay back by the end of the year. You'd better give up and go home," Oshima declared in an arrogant tone.

The woman, once considered a possible bride for Onoda by Oshima's aunt, was thus deprived of a chance to mention the debt owed her, and she stood alone watching the workmen. The woman had fled from her husband in the provinces and was renting a room in Tokyo. She brought her clothing and accessories with her and had a little money, and, for the first several months she spent in the city, she visited famous sites and lived off her savings. Then she started to provide for her daily expenses by working as a seamstress, a craft at which she was highly skilled. After a brief acquaintance, Oshima treated the woman as an old friend.

"Come and spend New Year's Eve with us," Oshima offered, violating the custom that it was the debtor bearing gifts who visited the lender on New Year's Eve.

The woman was appalled by this rudeness, and she left her seat across the brazier from Onoda and departed in silence.

"I know you don't like small talk, but there's no need to treat her like that," Onoda said, still trembling from the tension.

"If I hadn't been rude, we'd never have gotten rid of her." Oshima's voice was quivering as she explained. "Don't think I'm heartless. I behaved as I did because I know it'll bring the day I can show my true gratitude for her kindness."

69

FOR THE THREE MONTHS that they continued to obtain government orders, it seemed they could make a go of the business, but, by early April, the sewing machine's racket was heard only intermittently. Oshima's expectations for the new business were not panning out. At the end of both February and March, little remained after the workmen were paid. They owed rent, and the small loans borrowed to see them through one crisis or another were rolled over, resulting in greater debt.

"We're working for the benefit of our employees," Oshima said, scolding Onoda as she began to feel the pressure of not making ends meet. The cutting table, so busy during the winter, was now silent and tidy, and, with no workmen present, the shop seemed lonely and forlorn.

It was the time of year when double-flowered cherry blossoms were stuck into empty sake bottles to decorate the landlord's house. Onoda and Oshima were no longer permitted to use his telephone. He had sent them several eviction notices.

Onoda was playing Japanese chess in front of the shop with a workman who did not have the means to search for better employment because Oshima and Onoda had not paid his wages. When they tired of the game, they went inside and began a silly discussion about women. For Oshima, contemplating her situation, Onoda's carefree expression made him look like a fool.

"Is this what happens in most tailor shops?" she asked. "I expected something different." She was smiling, as if to quiet her anxiety.

"Not necessarily," Onoda replied with a grimace. He lay down using a padded iron holder as a pillow and appeared to expect a long interrogation.

The sight of her partner reclining in front of her enraged Oshima, and she picked up a large piece of wood, the length of a ruler, and hurled it at his curly haired head.

"Lazy bastard!" she exclaimed.

Onoda felt compelled to slap her chubby cheek, and Oshima, with red, teary eyes, fought back. The ferocious battle continued.

As Oshima bolted out of the house, she seethed with a hatred so dark and violent that murdering Onoda would not have satisfied her.

Soon, the pale Oshima was climbing the stairs to visit the rented room of the woman whose clothing she had once borrowed.

"It was a mistake to marry him. I misjudged him!" Oshima sobbed. "I thought I could turn him into something like a human being, a man, and I hustled to find the money to set him up in his own shop, but I was all wrong," she said, tears of regret streaming down her cheeks.

"I'm going to leave him. Living with that man is an insult to my womanhood!" It seemed that Oshima's noisy sobbing would never cease.

70

"WHAT'S WRONG WITH YOU?" the astonished woman finally asked. She was used to working in silence all day and did not speak until Oshima calmed down. "I thought you were working hard at your business. What's the problem?"

"I slave and toil, and it makes no difference. This woman has never been called lazy," Oshima replied as she wiped the tears from her eyes.

"But people say Western-style tailors earn huge profits. With both of you working, life should be easy," the woman said with a smile, though she was still preoccupied with her own sewing.

"He's the problem! The man's got some awful disease. I'm the kind of person that, once I decide to do something, I'll see it through no matter what. I'll never be compatible with that slow-witted sluggard from Nagoya!"

"Then why did you marry him?" the woman asked primly.

Oshima turned her teary face away with a snort of exasperation. She knew this woman was not capable of understanding her feelings.

"Tokyo's such a pleasant place," the woman continued. "I moved here because I couldn't get along with my mother-in-law in the provinces. Before I left, I suffered so much in silence. Much pleasanter being single. I enjoy life now. I'll never marry again."

With an expression that said "What on earth is this woman talking about?" Oshima stopped listening and thought about her own troubles. She tried to suppress the sobs that convulsed her, but her sense of the tragedy of her situation overcame her, and she could not contain her tears. She felt persecuted at every turn.

When Onoda lumbered into the room, Oshima was seated next to the woman, who quietly continued her sewing. Dried tears crusted her eyelashes.

"Why so depressed? I've told you it takes a couple of years to get a business off the ground. From now on, I'll take care of the work at home, and you promote the business outside," Onoda said as he sat down and took out his cigarettes. "There isn't enough profit in the subcontract from the Bureau of Clothing, so we're quitting it. Tomorrow, your job'll be collecting orders."

Oshima snorted contemptuously, but Onoda's idea of a woman dealer appealed to her.

"You'll be active outside the shop, and I'll manage things inside. We might make a go of the business."

"How can I solicit orders in these clothes?" Oshima objected, but she thought of the satisfaction to be gained from work that no woman had ever done before.

By the time she returned with Onoda, Oshima had calmed down. She viewed the prospect of the coming day's work with pride.

"I have to get busy. Can't afford to waste more time," she thought, and a fresh resilience came to her heart.

71

FROM LATE SPRING to early summer, the shop showed signs of prospering from the orders Oshima obtained, but, in July, August, and September, she found only a few repair jobs yielding little profit, and the sewing machine was once again silent.

In the beginning, Oshima took the sample book that Onoda had borrowed from another shop and visited former acquaintances near her parents' home. She returned with orders for work jackets and knee trousers worn over kimonos when riding bicycles. These first tests of Oshima's business ability proved that she was suited to the job.

In her sales excursions with her sample book, Oshima found an unexpected source of amusement in joking and trading banter with male dealers. Determining the quality of cloth, haggling over prices, taking measurements—in these normally masculine activities, Oshima developed a cheerful fluency that helped her forget her personal problems.

At a factory in Ōji, where industrial smokestacks rose in profusion, male supervisors surrounded the popular Oshima in the reception office.

"If you'd like, I can have the company order all our uniforms from you," whispered one of the men, intending to support Oshima.

"I'm afraid our business doesn't have the capital to fill such a large order," Oshima finally answered. She was on the verge of accepting the offer when it occurred to her that the shop did not have enough cloth to make the uniforms.

On more than one occasion, the couple lost potentially good customers because a lack of money and credit meant they could not obtain sufficient cloth.

"That's fine. You're a valued customer," Oshima was forced to reply in good humor when she went to deliver the finished goods and the customer requested that payment be deferred. It was painful for her to return and report this to Onoda, who was waiting impatiently for the money to buy more material, so she spent dull, uneasy hours making the rounds of other customers.

"They seem like honest people. I wonder why they didn't pay?" Oshima said. Avoiding the look of disappointment on Onoda's face, she was wrapping a customer's Inverness left for repair.

"This garment will sleep till winter," Oshima declared, as if to reassure herself. Pawning a customer's possession, the beautifully tailored Inverness, a model of its kind, was an act that frightened her, but she took the garment to a pawnshop that she was recently growing familiar with.

At night, exhausted from her trips around the city, Oshima slept soundly. Half in a dream, her weary mind sensed the heavy pressure of a male body against her. Onoda had napped most of the day.

72

OSHIMA'S SEARCH for customers led her farther and farther from home, and she returned late every night. She thus was not aware of Onoda's makeshift contrivances to keep the shop open. These finally failed, and, following Onoda's plan, the couple moved to the Tsukishima district of the Kyōbashi ward early in the winter.

After selling the shop furnishings, Onoda was left with just under

two hundred yen. He wanted to start a new business with this sum, and they moved to a house where the rent was cheaper, but their money was depleted more quickly than they expected. Several customers could not pay, and soon the couple was left without access to capital. The end of the year found them in more precarious and desperate circumstances than they had experienced the year before.

Day after day, dressed in a cheap coat and a gaudy muffler, Oshima would leave early in the morning and return in a daze, empty-handed after her visits to her debtors. Tired of never having enough to do and of not being paid on time when there was work, the young workman would be absent from the shop for several days at a time, looking for a better job.

This young man, named Kimura, was sent home from the front of the Russo-Japanese War because of illness. In the army, he was the favorite of the officers in his regiment and had been promoted rapidly over his fellow soldiers, but, on his return to Japan, he had lost the discipline and sobriety essential to the workman's ethic, and he took to drinking in teahouses and spending money on prostitutes. In debt, he stole materials from his employer and ran off with his friends' clothing. With no place to turn, he drifted into Onoda's shop, but, by then, he had sobered up and become the timid fellow he had been before the war.

At first, sewing in the shop, he would quake in fear at the mere glimpse of a policeman's shadow. He would have done almost anything for his savior, Oshima, but, during the day, he refused to go out to buy so much as a button. Because he would not attend roll calls of his army reserve unit, he was technically a deserter. His criminal status made him all the more timid.

That morning, in his bedding at breakfast time, he had heard a quarrel between Onoda and Oshima in their room that had set his weak nerves aquiver. He thought the fight had started over a personal problem, a frequent source of discord between the two, but it had escalated to include the couple's terrible economic situation.

"I'm not a beast you can work to death inside the house and outside, too," Oshima declared, raising her habitual complaint.

The couple then argued over who was responsible for keeping the workman on.

"If you'd just do your work, we wouldn't need an employee. The apprentice would be enough," argued the emotionally erratic Oshima.

The young man came to suspect that Oshima was heartless, the same Oshima who had once inspired him with the vow that she would protect him together with the shop no matter what happened.

73

KIMURA ROAMED THE CITY for two days looking for work, and, depressed and exhausted by his failure, he returned to the shop in the evening to find the place soaked with water.

Having gained nothing from his search for employment but the certain knowledge that ugly rumors about his sudden moral dissipation were circulating around tailor shops throughout the city, Kimura crossed over to the island on the cold, windswept ferry and walked to the neighborhood where Oshima had her shop. He intended to stay on a while longer with Oshima. Oshima was nowhere to be seen. Onoda was hard at work mopping up water that had inundated the room off the kitchen.

Meek but sturdily built, with thick lips and a prominent nose protruding from his tanned face, Kimura stood at the entrance and stared in amazement at the shop's condition. Screens, panels, and the floor were soaking wet.

"What happened? Was there a fire while I was gone?"

"Oshima's been up to her old tricks again. The woman's a monster," Onoda laughed.

From the evening of the previous day, Oshima, her eyes bloodshot, had stayed in bed. She complained of a headache. Her hair was a fright, and the rough skin of her face was as tense as stone. She occasionally groaned in pain.

The couple had recently been reduced to buying staples such as rice and soy sauce in small daily quantities. Oshima had barely eaten since morning and lay covered by the bedding she had miraculously held on to from the time of her marriage to Tsuru.

Onoda, doing the cooking and shopping himself, was irritated by the disorder that he encountered everywhere in the household, functioning as it was without a woman's guiding hand, but, at the same time, he was worried by the severity of Oshima's menstrual pain, evident from her moaning.

"The bones in my lower back are about to crack and break

apart," Oshima exclaimed, moving to cling to Onoda's arm. Her red, watery eyes fixed on him. Onoda spoke some comforting words and began massaging Oshima's lower back.

"I wonder if there's something physically wrong with me? I've never experienced such pain before. Perhaps my body is different? Do all women suffer like this?" As her back was being rubbed by Onoda, Oshima expressed some of the doubts troubling her. She went on to complain about something wrong with her sexual constitution or with Onoda's. She felt sorry for Onoda, but, at the same time, she had never imagined that marriage to him could inflict such pain.

The erotic association of Tsuru with her bedding led Oshima to bring up details of her physical relations with her former husband. This put Onoda in a bad humor. Oshima's outstretched hand resisting Onoda's pressing body suddenly whipped across his hot cheek.

The ferocious Oshima fled to the water tap and frantically turned the attached hose on Onoda to defend herself against his vengeance.

74

THE INSTANT ONODA FLINCHED and drew back, Oshima was out of the house. Her legs moving like the pistons of some wonderfully invigorated machine, Oshima strode rapidly through one neighborhood after another until she found herself moving in the direction of the waterfront.

As far as she could see, the long broad street, monotonous and ugly in the winter evening, was depressingly still and empty, yet a tremendous racket suffused her surroundings. The dark, vacant faces of men and women appeared here and there in the dim light of shops. Dispirited-looking factory workers streamed past her, and bicycle bells muffled by the wet air from the sea rang dully in her ears. Invisible white sand blown up from the street struck her face hard enough to hurt her eyes and cheeks, which were wet with tears.

The road brought her to a bridge. She wandered back and forth in front of it as if she were a vagrant woman searching for a place to die, but, from time to time, she walked out onto the structure to lean against the rail, resting there, breathing deeply to restore her body, tired from combat. Cold wind from the sea stung her white skin.

The colors of dusk approached, spreading over the expanse of water before her. Once she had calmed down enough to set back out for home, severe pain again wracked her lower back.

The neighborhood was dark when she returned. An old man whom she had never met was waiting at the entrance of the shop.

After exchanging a few words with the stranger, Oshima realized he was telling her that she had won the secret lottery she had bought into on an impulse, drawn to play by her love of speculation.

"You're sure to win," Kimura had insisted. "You've got a lucky aura about you."

Her nerves worn thin by worry over how to settle the shop's debts by the end of the year, Oshima was persuaded to take a chance by her young employee, who had knowledge of such matters. He was acquainted with a local house secretly taking bets.

"No! I won't lower myself. . . ." She was tempted but at first refused.

"Don't be so sure. Life's a gamble. But don't make a habit of it either. Once you've won, stop," Kimura urged.

"What should I bet on?"

"Whatever appeals to you. Something you've seen or heard. . . . Better yet if a dream guides you."

Oshima had seen a dragon in a dream the night before, so she put her money on the dragon.

Out of the blue, the old man had brought her two hundred yen, a completely unexpected windfall.

Secret joy spread over the hearts of Oshima, Onoda, and Kimura, who had been badly frightened by their economic situation.

"Something eerie in this, isn't there?" Oshima whispered to Onoda. Then she clapped her hands in prayer before the household shrine, where she had placed the money after the old man departed.

75

As if the fight had been completely forgotten, their eyes flashing with shared excitement, Oshima, Onoda, and Kimura sat together beneath a lantern glowing red-hot. Oshima thought that perhaps her fate was a rare and wonderful one, indeed. Light seemed to rise from the black depths of her mind.

"Things like this actually happen," Oshima exclaimed, her voice trembling with emotion. "What Kimura said was right. Maybe I'm the kind of person who can succeed only by playing for high stakes."

"A bighearted woman like you won't make it by following the herd," Kimura said.

"Maybe I should quit this complicated tailoring business and speculate on the stock market," she continued.

"That's right! There's no future for tailors. Looking for work these past couple of days, I've realized I hate this trade." Kimura hung his head and sighed.

"You don't know what you're talking about," Onoda muttered. "How are we going to start over in another business?"

Carried away by his own ideas, Kimura ignored his boss: "I think the days of the independent tailor shop are numbered. The times are against this crazy business. We're caught between the merchants selling Western fabrics and the seamsters. You're not really a merchant, and you're not really a craftsman either!" Kimura sounded excited.

"Why's that?" Oshima asked, wrinkles forming at the corners of her eyes in a smile. "Here we go again," she added under her breath.

"It's obvious," Kimura continued, surprised that the logic of his argument was not clear. "You make the customer wear outrageously expensive clothes, and the craftsman ends up working just to keep the shop afloat. Because your capital's always asleep, the small enterprise can't survive. The customer'd be better off buying the cloth directly from a clothier and giving it to a seamster to tailor!"

Her head tilted to the side, Oshima listened with great interest. She had thought Kimura a fool, but now he seemed a clever fellow with a new perspective on the problems that she faced.

"You're a workman, and you think like one! In real life, it isn't that simple," Onoda said with a contemptuous smile.

"But he's not stupid," Oshima concluded. "He seems headed for success."

She took down the bundle of bills from the family shrine, peeled off ten yen, and energetically headed for the entrance.

"Let me see it!" Eyes gleaming with greed, Onoda stretched the bill out in front of him. "Don't spend it all in one place!"

Soon the sake and tempura that Oshima had ordered arrived, and the men began drinking.

76

RUMORS THAT OSHIMA HAD WON the lottery soon spread through the neighborhood, and a local building contractor, boss of the Suzuki Company, ordered a coat to celebrate her good luck. From this fortuitous connection, prosperity suddenly came to the shop.

When Oshima went to take the order from this local boss, she dressed in new clothes. A cold rain was falling in Tsukishima, and the contractor had given his men the day off. Five of them were seated around the brazier. Replica toy rakes, symbolic of luck for raking in cash, had been bought at the Festival of Birds a few days earlier, and these decorated the huge family altar. New Year's gifts were piled high. Oshima recognized several of the men.

"I've heard you're quite a woman, so I'm going to have you make me an overcoat," the fiftyish boss declared as he opened the sample book. Gold teeth and rings gleamed on his body, and he was dressed in a heavily padded kimono. A stylish, thin woman in her late thirties sat next to him. She was wearing soft silk.

"If the clothing feels right, I'll send some paying customers your way," the boss offered, after casually ordering from the sample book and lighting his pipe. Oshima was commissioned to manufacture an overcoat with an otter-fur collar and a fur-lined waistcoat, items of clothing finer than anything she had created before. Without a second thought, Oshima gave an estimated price that would have caused most peoples' eyes to open wide in astonishment.

"We're honored that you'll be wearing our clothing, and please do recommend us to everyone you know. If we can obtain prominent citizens such as yourself as patrons, we'll surely succeed."

The men in the room were watching Oshima as she gave her speech, and they laughed in amusement.

"Is it true you do all the work and your husband stays at home and does nothing?" one of men asked.

"That's what everyone says," she replied, blushing as she put away her sample book. "A few customers have visited the shop when I wasn't there and couldn't place an order. So people have told me that it looks like I'm managing the place by myself."

Oshima went on talking for two hours, entertaining those present with the story of how she started her business.

"Ask around that neighborhood, and you'll see everyone's heard of my uncle Takishō. He was boss of the local gang. I still have customers in that world," Oshima confessed as she was about to leave.

77

FOR THE SHORT TIME that this sort of work continued, Oshima, dressed in her new clothes, spent her days making the rounds of customers. During the evenings, in the midst of the hustle and bustle at the end of the year, she and Onoda went out looking for fun in the lively town. Accompanying customers' wives with whom she had become friendly, Oshima would go to the theater or wander through the entertainment district of Asakusa. But this period of prosperity abruptly ended, and the couple was left again without work to spend their profitless days wondering what had become of the money they had squandered.

While Onoda and Oshima were out, Kimura did no more than the tasks assigned to him and was so occupied with designing a toy he had conceived that he often forgot to eat his meals.

During the day, in the intervals between sewing jobs, he was entirely wrapped up in his project. At times, he rustled around late at night long after the couple had gone to bed.

"What's our friend up to now?" Oshima asked with a grin, drawing close to Kimura, who was absorbed in a corner of the room in cutting out cardboard, pasting, and coloring.

"I'm fiddling around with this," Kimura replied without looking up. Pieces of cardboard were sculpted in fine detail, and he was drawing dice-like patterns on them and placing them in order.

"What's the thing that looks like a ticket?"

"That one?" Kimura said, still absorbed in his work. "That's a warship."

"What'll you do with a warship?"

"I'm making a naval chess set."

"A naval chess set? What for?"

"I plan to make a lot of money with this sophisticated new game. The small piece is a torpedo boat."

"You have strange ideas. Trying to profit off the war with Russia, huh?"

"That's right. When this game catches on, I'll lend you huge sums of capital! I'm the sort of person who doesn't need much money."

"That'll be wonderful." Oshima burst out laughing.

"This isn't my only idea." Recently, the young workman hardly slept at night, his mind awhirl with a number of clever projects. Enthusiasm for his creations caused his timid heart to beat more rapidly.

"I've enjoyed inventing things ever since I was a child, and I have a number of other plans. One or two of them are bound to succeed," Kimura continued.

"So you're trying to become an inventor. I've always had great admiration for inventors, but, if it's the kind of thing you can do, I guess I don't admire them much any more!" Oshima declared.

"It's no joke," Kimura insisted.

"There's nothing wrong with invention. Just keep up with the shop's work, too. I'm going out now to collect lots more for you to do!" Oshima countered.

78

ON THEIR RETURN TO Tokyo after a six-month residence in the flourishing city of Nagoya, close to Onoda's hometown, Onoda and Oshima had no place to stay, and they became live-in employees in a tailor shop in the Tsukiji district of the Kyōbashi ward, Onoda hired as a workman and Oshima as a saleswoman.

From January to March, the couple found they could no longer keep their business afloat, and they closed their shop in Tsukishima and, relying on a tailor friend who had already emigrated, set off for Shanghai in China. They stopped to pay a brief visit in Onoda's hometown but were caught in the quagmire of Nagoya while trying to raise money for travel expenses.

About the time Oshima and Onoda closed their shop in Tsukishima, Kimura, who had over the previous three months developed various ideas he hoped to patent, discovered that similar ideas had already been patented or that he could not afford the fees. Discouraged, he abandoned his inventions and again fell into the world of transient workmen.

In Nagoya, a littler closer to the East China Sea, which they planned to cross to reach the continent, the couple unpacked their meager possessions at the house of Onoda's sister and her husband, an office worker. Onoda still had many acquaintances in the area. They had hoped to stay with his sister for several days and then, after visiting Onoda's father, who lived in a village about five miles away, leave from there. In the meantime, however, Onoda had visited his father and found that the old man, who had lost his former house and lands, was living as an impoverished peasant. Onoda was ashamed to have Oshima meet this pitiful old man. Grown accustomed to Tokyo, even Onoda was repelled by his father's shabby life.

They had hoped that the father might provide them with travel expenses if he met Oshima, and at least twice Oshima insisted that Onoda take her with him to see the old man. Onoda looked uncomfortable and refused.

Eight or nine years before, Onoda's alcoholic father was widowed, losing his hardworking, intelligent wife, and since then his life had become daily more chaotic. While the wife could still work, they somehow held on to their house, but it had been mortgaged time and again, and it had finally been repossessed by the bank. Now he barely survived, living alone in a small shack.

In the end, Onoda took Oshima to see his father, and they found him digging in the dirt of a mountain field producing barley and fava beans. When Oshima saw the old man's ignorant-looking expression and his dirty skin burned dark by the sun, she experienced such a shock that she began to shiver. Contempt for Onoda froze her heart.

79

Now Oshima understood why Onoda had not brought her face-to-face with his father before. They returned to Nagoya the same day, ignoring the old man's obvious disappointment. Oshima felt that she had been deceived and was furious. But she also found the situation comical when she considered how Onoda had explained her to his father.

Broad flowing fields of green barley and mulberry stretched out before her. She saw peasants and their horses plowing muddy rice paddies. Oshima and Onoda were returning to Nagoya in a slow, horse-drawn cart surrounded by dust from the white dirt road. Onoda, drunk from the unrefined sake that his father urged on him, was dozing in the back of the cart. Oshima gazed down with pity at his large head and closely cropped hair.

Entering the city after experiencing the impoverished village, Oshima found her surroundings, which had seemed to her so backward and desolate on her arrival, now seemed lively and prosperous. A large Western-style building caught her eye, and she looked about in admiration at the beautiful shops, finer than any she had seen in Tokyo, and the fashionable restaurants. The quiet neighborhood where Onoda's sister lived contained estates with gates and gardens so grand they made Oshima curious about the people residing there.

According to Onoda, his father still owned a small hill, and, when he sold this last piece of property, he would have money to lend them. Oshima was to do everything she could to please the old man so he would give them the money.

"With a plan like that, we'll never get out of here," Oshima argued that night upstairs in Onoda's sister's house. The room was often let to office workers or students from other provinces to supplement the family's meager income. Oshima could see the tinted glow of electric lights from a movie house and the local theater. Young leaves below the window grew daily more verdant. The noisy songs of frogs in distant paddies made Oshima melancholy. The couple arrived prepared for spring, but the weather had turned quite warm. Wearing only a white shirt, Onoda was stretched out on the floor. He believed that, with luck, he and Oshima could lead an interesting life in his native city. A journey to faraway Shanghai now seemed folly—perilous and exhausting.

"Absolutely not! Success in a provincial city is no success at all. It's nothing I can brag about when I return to Tokyo," Oshima argued, rejecting Onoda's idea. In Oshima's fantasies, the trip to Shanghai, where money was rolling in the streets, was gilded with the prestige of a journey to the West.

80

BY THE TIME THE COUPLE had left Nagoya and returned to Shinbashi in Tokyo, they had nothing but the clothes on their backs. Arriving on a hot summer evening, they had no place to spend the night.

Among the cordial but wary citizens of Nagoya, the fast-talking Oshima was seen as a strange interloper, coldly rejected wherever she went. Onoda had found a job for a couple of months as a live-in workman in a tailor shop. Oshima seemed to spend almost as much time there as he, though she was despised as a disruptive nuisance. Because of Oshima's frank speech and loose, spendthrift ways, Onoda's sister and her friends regarded her as a sort of female swindler. At first, while the sister still trusted Oshima to do her hair in the latest Tokyo fashion or help her with the washing and sewing, she begrudged Oshima little, loaning her hair ornaments, other accessories, and small sums of money. In time, however, the sister discovered that she should be cautious in her dealings with Oshima.

"Don't be so stingy! We'll soon make a bundle and pay you back with loads of interest," Oshima answered with a laugh when refused a loan by the sister, but she was angered at the thought that these provincials believed they had seen through her. It vexed her that her actions and intentions were so misunderstood.

They were stuck in this place where Onoda had built up no trust or credit and Oshima herself had no experience with local business customs. It seemed their resolve to set out for Shanghai was weakening by the day. Having saved enough of Onoda's wages to cover their traveling expenses, the almost penniless couple finally boarded a train for Tokyo. Exhausted by the stifling heat in the crowded passenger car, Onoda and Oshima were pushed out into the quiet square in front of the station.

"Where'll we go now?" Oshima sighed, prodding Onoda, crouched next to her under an advertising tower with flashing red and blue lights. The soft evening air had revived her.

Onoda was considering Kawanishi's factory, where he had once been employed, but he had borrowed wages in advance and had not worked the sum off and was reluctant to go back. He had boasted to his fellow workers that he was emigrating to Shanghai, and he was ashamed to appear before them.

81

THEY SPENT AN UNEASY NIGHT at a cheap inn near the station. The next day, they wandered the steaming city searching for employment, until Kawanishi took them in.

After visiting several shops in the Hongō ward, the couple lost all hope, and, as the sun set, they retreated to the Yushima shrine to rest beneath a tree, as if they were starving vagrants.

In the dim light of the gathering dusk within the shrine's grounds, they saw a number of human figures gathered around benches and arbors. Autumn-like clouds moving through the sky were visible between the yellow-tinged leaves of cherry trees and the branches of ginkgo trees. The buildings in the city below seemed drained by the long summer's heat. Onoda and Oshima stopped to rest on a bench in the faint shadow of a tree. A cool breeze flitted pleasantly across their tired, sunburned faces.

The pale color of night, translucent as water, slowly spread to the edges of the surrounding stands of trees. Sitting there in silence, Oshima suddenly spied a crippled, leprous beggar crawling up the stone steps of the gentler slope to the level ground of the shrine.

When he reached the top step, the pitiful, ugly beggar surveyed his surroundings timidly, like a mud turtle emerging on land, and then started crawling on his knees again. In search of lodging for the night, he dragged himself over to a small abandoned shrine in the darkest area of the grounds.

"Look at that!" Oshima exclaimed, turning to Onoda.

Onoda, who had been smoking, was asleep, his body supported by the arm of the bench.

"You're hopeless," she said, her voice rising. "Let's get out of here. We can't stay a moment longer!" Oshima woke Onoda and stood up trembling.

"We'll go to Kawanishi's in Shiba. In our present situation, there's no sense in false pride," she said, forcing her exhausted husband to come to a decision. Their aching legs leaden, they moved on.

They had eaten nothing since lunch and were too tired and hungry to speak. It was about nine o'clock in the evening.

82

AFTER THEIR DIFFICULT, fruitless journey to Nagoya, Oshima and Onoda were surprised by Kawanishi's generosity in taking them in so readily. There were no more government orders from the Bureau of Clothing, so many workmen and salesmen had been laid off, and the shop seemed depressingly empty.

Oshima discovered a middle-aged divorcée working in the kitchen. The woman was acting as a housekeeper for the bachelor Kawanishi, and Oshima helped out energetically, if not particularly efficiently.

Where the woman came from no one knew, but a workman had brought her into the formerly all-male shop, and soon there was talk about the boss's relationship with her. She was small of stature, urbane in fashion, with an ignorant-looking face of dark complexion. After Oshima came to live in the shop, the woman was even more careful to look her best and to fulfill the duties of the woman of the house, occupying the wife's customary seat by the brazier.

His days spent busily supervising all aspects of the shop's operations, Kawanishi went upstairs to bed with the setting sun, but he was up early in the morning while his woman still slept. His foul-mouthed workmen and apprentices gossiped behind his back about their generous but nagging boss.

Oshima was up before the woman, too, and she briskly cleaned the downstairs rooms and supervised the serving of breakfast. By the time the sleepy-looking woman came down with a smile on her loose face, the workmen had finished their breakfast and were gossiping about her as they worked in the shop at the back of the house.

While the men were eating, Oshima went out back to do the laundry. She took the clean garments up to a platform constructed over the roof and hung them on poles under the high sun.

"I'm sorry to trouble you with the wash," the woman apologized in a languid voice. At the upstairs window, she stood gazing at Oshima working energetically beneath the blazing sun. The woman looked thin, dressed in only a crumpled patterned sleeping robe and red undergirdle, with her fine hair done back. Dabs of white face powder on her forehead highlighted by reflected sunlight made her appear dirty.

"It's no trouble," Oshima replied, ducking under the clothing hung out to dry. She wiped the perspiration from her face with her sleeve. "I'm the sort of person who isn't satisfied unless I'm working. No amount of work bothers me," she continued.

"Is that so?" the woman muttered, her dark eyes revealing that she was still lost in a pleasant dream. "I usually don't go to sleep until midnight or one," she added.

"That's fine, Ohide. Your superior station in life allows you to do as you please. Everyone says so!"

The woman reddened and frowned.

"I'm sorry!" Oshima said. "You must be offended by my use of your first name."

83

IF A DAY PASSED and she was unable to go out, Oshima felt frustrated. The workmen had nothing to do, so, for the first time in several days, the cheerful Oshima left at noon carrying her sample book.

"I've found you a splendid customer!" Oshima called out to Kawanishi and Ohide as she returned in the evening.

As she was leaving, Oshima looked around the quiet shop and concluded that her efforts kept the establishment afloat, and it was true that Oshima would always come back with orders even though Kawanishi had no new prospects for customers. Oshima and Onoda looked through the orders that she had taken among her own acquaintances, and, on the excuse that some were too small for the shop to handle, the couple filled them themselves, pocketing the profit. Kawanishi was not pleased when he saw Onoda working on private jobs when the shop was idle.

"You're doing a great job, but your abilities are wasted on that man," Kawanishi commented at the end of a discussion with Oshima about a new customer. He had sent the apprentice off with the bicycle on an errand to Kyōbashi. Kawanishi, now in his mid-forties, had expanded his business by producing ready-made Western-style clothing and contracting with the Bureau of Clothing and other institutions, but, since Oshima and Onoda's arrival, he had been gaining orders for custom-tailored garments.

Reeking of sake, Kawanishi told Ohide, who had served him dinner, that she could go to the public bath before him. The workmen and apprentices had gone in search of entertainment in the town, and the shop was empty.

"With your talents, it's beyond me why you'd go all the way to Nagoya," Kawanishi remarked, repeating what he had said to her before.

"It was awful. I should've left Onoda then and there, but I guess we're fated to stay together," Oshima replied.

"I know you and Onoda plan to leave with the customers you've found for me and set up your own shop, but you'll find it difficult with Onoda's skills as a tailor."

"Don't I know! We've failed time and again."

"Why don't you divorce Onoda and come make some real money with me?" Kawanishi proposed with a leer.

"Surely you're joking," Oshima replied, blushing. "You have Ohide."

"Who'd marry a thing like that? Nobody knows what cat dragged her in," Kawanishi declared with a sneering cackle.

"But she's such a nice person. You must take good care of her. A selfish woman like me is no good for you," Oshima exclaimed, withdrawing to the shop to change her sweaty clothes. The humid shop was meticulously tidy. The harsh electric lights illuminated the room.

84

At about nine in the evening, Onoda returned and found a frightened Oshima still in a state of agitation. She was both ashamed and indignant that a coarse man of Kawashima's low character would even consider her the sort of woman he could have his way with at any time or place.

"Do you really think I'm that kind of woman? What would my strict father say if I did that with you!" Oshima scolded Kawanishi, who had chased her into a corner, where she cringed, trembling in fear. She had resisted the man's powerful and violent advances across the full length of the shop floor. With his long, unshaved chin and sunken eyes, Kawanishi reminded Oshima of a madman.

"You mustn't! This is my precious body! I have to succeed, but I won't if I don't save my honor!" she insisted, brusquely slapping away his muscular hands. There was a fierce struggle.

Muttering that a woman who lacked delicacy and feminine grace was an insult to his manhood anyway, Kawanishi angrily stormed upstairs. As she rubbed her injured elbow, Oshima felt the harsh anxiety of a proud, victorious woman.

The heavily powdered Ohide returned from the public bath to find Oshima standing, arms folded, in front of the shop. She smiled at Oshima and passed through the entrance.

"Stupid woman," Oshima thought, and she remained silent, not bothering to look at Ohide. This dully satisfied woman, so easily intimidated, irritated Oshima beyond words.

"When Onoda returns, I'll tell him everything that's happened. Both of us are leaving here tonight!" she concluded and remained outside waiting. A cold autumn breeze sprang up. Passing figures and the lights from surrounding shops seemed muted and isolated. She sadly remembered Tsuru and the young master of the Hamaya.

That night, Onoda quarreled with Kawanishi upstairs. He finally came down, a worried expression on his face, and announced, "He says that he doesn't have enough work to keep us on. He's sorry for us but wants us to leave now."

Oshima snorted. Her nerves were still on edge, and she was not in the mood for a detailed conversation about the events of the evening.

"He seemed angry about our doing our own work," Onoda added.

"Of course that's what he'd say!" Oshima grumbled and laughed derisively. "Let's get out of here. I was planning to quit even if he didn't fire us."

85

EARLY THE NEXT MORNING, Oshima roused the vacillating Onoda to go out and find them a place to live.

"Did you do something to make the boss angry?" Onoda had asked Oshima reproachfully the night before when they were alone in their room. This morning he was still bothered by the same doubts.

"What would I say to him?" she answered, frowning in irritation. She had meant to speak frankly about the incident, but, now that they were leaving anyway, she was not inclined to bring it up. "I think I've worked hard and done my best for his shop."

"But you did say something, didn't you?" Onoda interjected.

"Leave me alone, will you?" Oshima replied, forehead furrowing in anger. "I can't play up to that animal the way you do—'Yes sir,' 'Yes sir,' 'Yes sir!'"

"See! You take that tone, and there's bound to be trouble. Your problem is your attitude!" Onoda countered.

"You're much dumber than I am. You let Kawanishi make a fool of you. Find a backbone, and be a man!"

Searching the Shiba ward for half a day, they finally found a six-by nine-foot room for rent at the back of a printer's shop in the Atago district. They used up most of the little money they had to rent the place and moved in the same day.

The printer's shop was cozy and attractive. To prevent Onoda from being tempted by amusements, Oshima immediately went in search of orders from prospective customers. Onoda left for Kawanishi's to negotiate the cheap rental of a sewing machine, but he returned disappointed and somewhat angry. Oshima was waiting for him with several garments to repair.

"You see, people are sympathetic to us. I found orders almost at once. If you work hard, we'll succeed here!" she bragged as soon as Onoda came in. Oshima's tireless resistance and animosity toward others had given birth to an unusual resilience in her.

The electric lights had come on, and Oshima was noisily preparing dinner in the small kitchen. She was already on familiar terms with the woman owner of the print shop.

"What happened with the sewing machine?" Oshima asked.

"We'll get nothing out of Kawanishi. He speaks very poorly of you. He said I should divorce you."

"The evil bastard!" Oshima declared, tilting her head to the side. "So the animal still hates me. But we've got to get our hands on a sewing machine."

As soon as dinner was finished, Oshima set off for a nearby sewing-machine company and ordered one. When the machine was delivered the next morning, they were able to get back to work.

86

AFTER MOVING to the small room, Oshima and Onoda would go out together in the evening like newlyweds.

Since leaving Kawanishi's shop, affection had rekindled between them, and, now with a substantial monthly income at their disposal, they would dress in the new clothing that they had made for the cooler weather and attend vaudeville halls or other lively entertainments.

At first in the new shop, Oshima had only the clothes on her back, for, in her various moves, she had either given her kimonos away, sold them for next to nothing, or worn them out. As soon as Oshima was able to anticipate future profit, however, she went to a clothier whom she had known in Tsukishima and brought back material so gaudy it made Onoda dizzy. Sewing her kimono herself, Oshima used Onoda as a mannequin.

"We can't afford new clothes yet. Buying kimonos we haven't budgeted for will cause problems in the future," warned Onoda, who cared little about clothing. Oshima criticized Onoda for wasting money in a neighborhood beer hall, where he listened to the phonograph and flirted with waitresses, but, when it was a matter of her own indulgences, she often ignored the budget that she had drawn up.

"When I remember you're the son of that old man in Nagoya, I feel sick! Maybe you'd have turned out like him if you hadn't come to Tokyo," Oshima suggested, leering broadly and laughing as she stared at Onoda.

"Nonsense," Onoda replied. He stroked the mustache that he had recently started to grow.

"Then stop flirting with women in the beer hall and mind the business so you can buy me a few nice clothes. I despise men who play around with those kind of women. They'll damage your character," Oshima continued. She spoke with force, as if to drive away the image of his father that lurked behind some of Onoda's cruder facial expressions. The resemblance was particularly strong when Onoda was eating or laughing.

"What's so strange about a child's looking like his parent? I'm no bastard," Onoda replied. He hid his indignation with a strained smile.

"I won't say you'd have been better off as a bastard, but you certainly don't want to resemble your father!" Oshima insisted.

"That's a cruel thing to say. I owe a great debt to my parents," Onoda asserted, his voice finally revealing his anger.

"I admire that about you. You can respect a parent like that. If he were my father, I'd deny it."

87

As Oshima's antipathy toward Onoda and his father became more pronounced, she felt that she could never succeed, no matter how she struggled, with such a partner. His features began to seem common. The character of a man who enjoyed the company of beerhall women was clearly inferior.

"I won't allow a woman to insult my parents!" Onoda declared, furious, and returned to the sewing machine, working the pedal in silence.

Since she did not have the money to make the monthly payment for the machine, the cunning Oshima had told the salesman that it was defective, and a replacement requiring a trial period was delivered, again deferring the deadline for payment.

"If we don't take these risks, we'll never succeed!" Oshima said then, proud of her cleverness. But now the sight of Onoda sitting at the machine, taking its possession for granted, made her efforts seem ridiculous.

The clattering of the device stopped, and Onoda placed the garment on the cutting table and ironed the seam.

"What an idiot!" she sighed, folding her arms across her chest. An irrational anger rose within her.

"You're going to end your life as a mere workman, just another wage slave. I suppose that's a little better than your peasant father slogging around in the mud of his rice paddies," Oshima declared.

"So you know everything! Your parents are so superior! Doesn't your father make a living by fiddling around in the dirt?"

"Who went to those same parents and begged to marry me? My father may not look like much now, but he's wellborn. He used to lord it over the district as the village headman. Still, I've never bragged about my family."

"Because you're an unfilial daughter and your parents won't let you near them. There's no profit in your pride. Go home, bow and apologize a little, and figure out a way to get some money out of them."

Onoda repeated what he had been urging Oshima to do for some time.

"Don't ask me to act like a cowardly hypocrite! Even in death I wouldn't approach my family unless I had my own shop facing the main street in broad daylight."

"See, as I've always said, you don't have the instinct to succeed in business."

As they were finishing up the day's tasks, Oshima and Onoda became absorbed once again in a discussion of their shop's future.

88

BEFORE LEAVING FOR NAGOYA on their way to Shanghai, Onoda and Oshima, bearing gifts, visited Oshima's parents. At the urging of Onoda, Oshima subsequently made several calls in an effort to win support from her parents.

"My father told me that this area around here will be my part of his inheritance," Oshima mentioned during the couple's first visit. She led Onoda around about a third of an acre, divided in several plots and densely planted with trees and shrubs.

A number of the plants were to be used in decorative gardens, but there were also groves of bamboo and untended fields. Several new houses had been built bordering directly on the property. Onoda stared in astonishment and entered one of the stands of trees. Trees were so thick that light could not penetrate, and the earth was damp beneath the rich growth of summer grasses.

"How much do you think the property's worth these days?" Onoda asked when he returned to Oshima's side. His eyes were glinting as he calculated.

"I really don't know," Oshima answered, feigning innocence. "Perhaps five thousand yen." She did not believe that the land would ever come into her possession.

Oshima's older brother, Sōtarō, who had been away from home

for many years, had finally returned from Chiba prefecture after his lover died. His wife, bringing his children, arrived from her parents' house and was living with her husband for the first time in many years. Sōtarō suffered from a terrible illness. His health damaged, he had none of the energy that he had displayed while living with Oshima in the mountains in Shiobara. Oshima remembered the days in the mountains when she became acquainted with Sōtarō's lover. The woman, infected by the same disease as Sōtarō, was pursued at every turn by her lover and died during her journey without knowing a moment's happiness. As Oshima objectively watched the development of the love affair between her brother and the woman, she thought she understood some of the emotions shared by the couple, but she still questioned what the woman saw in her brother that made her suffer so for him.

"Sōtarō certainly treated me badly that time." Oshima spoke as though her experiences with him had forced her to despair of ever feeling close to her wayward brother.

Her brother pretended not to remember their time together in Shiobara. He seemed displeased that Oshima and Onoda were approaching the family again.

"Sōtarō isn't a bad person. He just doesn't give a damn about the feelings of others," she told Onoda.

"What you should be worrying about is getting the deed to that land rewritten in your name!" Onoda said, irritated by Oshima's negligence.

"I don't know the status of the property now. But my mother won't let me get my hands on it while she's still alive."

"Because you've handled the situation poorly," Onoda retorted as they walked toward the entrance of the house. He seemed full of hope.

89

WHILE ONODA WAS ABSORBED in earnest conversation with Oshima's mother, attempting to gain her trust, Oshima, to dispel her prickling sense of annoyance, went off to play with the children and talk loudly with her sister-in-law.

"Oshima's caused this family more trouble than any of the other children. I don't know how many times she's run away and come back home," the mother told Onoda while Oshima was still present.

Her mother judged Onoda the most reliable of the men whom Oshima had had relationships with. With his sturdy features and full mustache, Onoda could impress people as a splendid gentleman when he chose to. In his newly tailored Western-style suit, his natural lethargy gave him an air of dignity.

Before she departed for Nagoya, Oshima, in character, boasted to her parents that Onoda was from a family of wealthy provincial landowners. Onoda maintained this illusion in his conversation with the mother.

"His family's quite wealthy," Oshima declared again in front of her assembled family. She wanted to browbeat her mother, and Onoda took care not to contradict her.

"My family isn't that wealthy. But I don't think Oshima and I will struggle for long. If we earn people's trust, we should manage fine," he added, to gain the confidence of Oshima's mother.

Oshima could not sit still and listen to any more of this. She felt contempt for Onoda's sly hypocrisy, but she was also angered by her mother's gullibility in believing Onoda.

Sōtarō's wife told Oshima in confidence that her husband's land had been heavily mortgaged owing to his five years of dissipation.

"Father once said he was going to give me some land. What do you think he intends to do?" Oshima asked, putting out a feeler to her sister-in-law.

"Did you have that arrangement? I don't know a thing," the sister-in-law answered.

"I understand the men's shares have already been decided," Oshima continued.

When she thought of the respectable shop she could exchange for the property, Oshima desired it more than anything she ever had before. Still, she had to admit that her father had become estranged from her since she departed for the mountains.

"Come on, let's go!" she pressed Onoda, who was still talking to her mother, and they returned home.

90

THEIR CRAMPED LIFE in that small room and some physical abnormality in either Onoda or Oshima herself that would not allow Onoda to achieve sexual fulfillment at times put Oshima under terrible stress.

"Is that the truth?" the shocked Oshima asked the mistress of the printing shop. This older woman was married to a young husband and had occasion to teach Oshima about sexual relations between men and women.

"Could I be deformed?" Oshima inquired, thinking of the pain she experienced in satisfying Onoda's unnatural desire.

"It never happened before him, not once." Oshima, who spoke frankly with the older woman about the most intimate details, was ashamed to admit that she had had experience with previous husbands.

"To tell the truth, he's not my first," she confessed.

"Then it's probably your husband's fault," the older woman offered.

"But he says I'm to blame, so I believed him. . . . I felt sorry for him."

"Such a crazy thing isn't physically possible. Have a doctor take a look," the older woman suggested. She mentioned a number of other people's cases and treated Oshima's concerns as groundless obsessions.

"I'd be too embarrassed," Oshima stammered, reddening to the tips of her earlobes. She had contempt for the immodesty of this lewd older woman with her young husband, but she could not forget her worries about the problem. It even occurred to her that a wretched sexual life would doom Onoda and her to unhappiness together. In the morning, she would wake to find her whole body swollen and painful. On such occasions, Oshima often stayed in bed groaning. How she despised the weakness of the man whose aroused nerves kept him awake almost to dawn.

"Have to get busy!" Remembering customers she had to visit, she leaped out of bed and began preparing to go out. As if exhausted from a prolonged battle, Onoda sat stupidly in front of the cutting table, his dazed, sleepy eyes squinted shut against the bright sunlight.

"Shall I fix you up with a pretty young thing?" the older woman said in response to Onoda's joking request that she find him a mistress. "Then Oshima's chores would be reduced, and she'd have an easier life."

"That's nonsense. We're not nearly prosperous enough to keep a mistress," Oshima declared in anger, unwilling to ignore the woman's remark.

91

DURING THE SIX MONTHS the couple occupied the cramped quarters in Atago, they earned about two thousand yen. On opening their new shop in the Nezu district of the Hongō ward, Oshima's interest in promoting her business in the city was reinvigorated. From time to time, she would question close friends concerning doubts about her sexuality, but mostly these were dispelled in her busy daily activities.

With the pressure and disappointment resulting from the lack of sexual compatibility between the couple, thoughts of Tsuru and the young master of the Hamaya came alive again in Oshima's heart.

"Once I succeed, I'll pay a visit to the Hamaya in the mountains." This secret desire raised the prospect of extraordinary pleasures in her imagination as she made the rounds of her customers. There would be the satisfaction of gaining revenge on Onoda, who said he wanted a mistress, but she also longed for the joy and fulfillment that seemed to be missing from her present married life.

She also thought of Tsuru, who had found few prospects in the provinces and had returned to Tokyo to work for a wholesaler of Western wines and liquors. From her sister, she learned that Oyū had fled her husband and the old-fashioned Uegen house, which was in constant turmoil, and joined Tsuru. Still, Oshima was convinced she would meet her former husband again.

Oshima also felt she might meet a man other than Tsuru or the master of the Hamaya, a man outside Onoda's sphere of activity. In her rough, hard heart starving for success and action, there was still room for romantic yearning and disappointment.

From the tales of romance that she heard from the various women she met while searching out business connections—women such as her who were active in a trade, independent women, wives—Oshima had received the sure intimation that she, too, was a woman, and she had occasion to lose herself in secret longings and fantasies. At times, she felt that even her remarkable energy could not help her attain her shadowy desires.

"I really don't like you," she told Onoda. After she had been forced to bear the physical pain of sexual intercourse, resentment toward the man coursed through her body.

Although she had regarded the older woman at the printing shop as an enemy after the woman offered to find Onoda a mistress, she soon forgot the perceived insult. Oshima visited her after the move to Nezu and complained of the pain she suffered.

"Please find Onoda a mistress. If I don't get some relief, I won't be able to continue working," Oshima requested in all seriousness.

"You're joking! A mistress would be the start of your real problems."

The woman believed that Oshima's accounts of her relations with Onoda were simply fabrications.

92

THE COUPLE MOVED to Nezu because the Tokyo Exhibition of Commerce and Industry had opened there and had brought unprecedented prosperity to the district.

Their shop was located in a normally quiet, sleepy neighborhood, but the nearby exhibition had brought the raucous, lively street bands and group tours from the provinces searching for temporary lodgings.

With the arrival of fair weather, Onoda wrote a polite letter of invitation to his father, and the old man, tired of daily fieldwork in the provinces, came to Tokyo to see the sights. Similarly, Oshima sent letters to all her friends in Shiobara, and soon they were noisily crowding into the new shop. Prosperous times had come, and Oshima and Onoda saw nothing wrong in celebrating.

The couple took Onoda's father, who knew nothing of the struggle required to establish his son's shop, to the exhibition soon after he arrived, and he was deeply moved by the sights. Oshima was able to participate in the father's wonder and gained a certain satisfaction in obliging this pitiful old man, who had never seen one interesting thing in his life.

The leaves of the trees in Ueno park had turned a darker green. Day after day, the humid heat of the rainy season or shadows from gloomy rain clouds covered the masses, gathering like ants from all directions. Almost every day, Oshima would put on her new summer coat, and Onoda would don his panama hat, and the couple would take the old man out on amusing excursions in the city. On occasion, however, Onoda's granting his father's every whim caused Oshima to doubt her self-sacrifice. The ignorant old man would stop and stare at something, and the stupidly filial Onoda would wait as patiently as a doting husband, refusing to leave his father's side. No matter how vulgar or silly the attraction, when the old man's eyes widened in wonder, Onoda would happily follow his father to explain.

"We're not wealthy enough to spend day after day entertaining your father," Oshima complained. She was in her bedding, her palms pressed against her temples, when Onoda came upstairs to scold her. It was customary for the son's wife to serve her father-in-law sake at dinner, but Oshima refused and withdrew to her bed as if seriously ill. As often occurred during her menstrual period, she was writhing in pain, suffering as though on the border between life and death.

"In this physical condition, I can't possibly wait on your father," she groaned.

93

"DO YOU MEAN THAT?" Onoda asked, his expression taking Oshima to task. He tugged at his mustache, a sign that he was growing angry. Oshima's departure just as his father was beginning to enjoy himself was an affront to Onoda's dignity.

Oshima remained in bed scowling, but, after the forlorn Onoda went downstairs, she was overcome by anger at his father's inability to understand the difficulties she had undergone in building up the business. She was no longer the center of attention, and her failure to show the old man what she was made of brought on selfish tears of frustration.

Restless, Oshima descended to find the father already drinking. The dejected Onoda sat beside him. Still frowning, she approached the old man, who was sitting at a small table with nothing on it to eat.

"I'm sorry, but when I'm ill like this, I can't manage anything. Our trade falls off in the summer, and I'm afraid we can't offer you more hospitality," she apologized.

"Don't give it a second thought. I'm not really a guest but part of the family," the father replied, hinting at his desire to continue living with the couple until he died. Not satisfied with the stingy last serving of sake that Oshima poured for him, and driven by a craving for alcohol, the old man staggered out to drink at a local bar he had recently begun frequenting. This mean drinking habit that could not be contained quietly within the house caused Oshima to hold the barbaric old man in even greater contempt.

94

AFTER THE ARRIVAL of five of Oshima's friends from Shiobara, Onoda's father became more of a nuisance.

Among the guests was the young master of the Hamaya, who had contracted a respiratory disease. He had come to Tokyo to be examined by specialists as well as to view the sights. Also in the group were the woman owner of the hot-spring resort in the mountains and the rice miller. The miller traveled to Tokyo once a month to observe the rice market in the Kakigara district. This time he brought his wife and children.

Oshima received a postcard informing her that her friends had arrived, and, in the evening, she had the apprentice wrap up a present of a large box of cakes, and she set off with her hair done in a matronly style and wearing a crested summer kimono. Her friends had crowded into a single room of an inn and were talking in loud, cheerful voices as they prepared to start the evening's drinking.

"What a successful, self-made woman! And you're prettier than ever. A beautiful young wife!" the miller, sitting in the middle of the room, declared as Oshima entered the room.

"You're teasing!" Oshima answered, but she felt herself blushing like an innocent girl.

"Somehow we've managed to survive, but we're still a long way from success. Tailoring requires a great deal of capital, and I was wondering whether this gathering of prosperous ladies and gentlemen would consider investing in our business!" she declared, bringing laughter from all present. The merry room became even more animated with Oshima's arrival.

Oshima left the crowded inn before the group was scheduled to depart on a nighttime tour of the city. She carefully instructed them how to find her shop, and they parted, her friends seeing her off to the street.

"They say you're ill. What's wrong?" Oshima asked as she walked beside the young owner of the Hamaya. She had planned, if necessary, to borrow capital from him. Her brother, who retained connections with gardeners in the region, had informed her of the rumor that the young man had recently struck it rich speculating in mountain properties. She knew he might have money to invest.

"I'm not really ill. They told me to be careful because I have weak lungs, so I consulted with specialists here in Tokyo. I'll stay for a while to see the sights and receive injections."

"I suppose you've caught your wife's disease. Glad I didn't stay with you!" Oshima said, feigning terror, but she could not treat the young man as a consumptive. "Don't worry. If you do come down with lung disease, I'll nurse you back to health. I'm not afraid of lung disease."

"If you're susceptible, you've caught it already, so it's too late for caution now. Besides, you're the one who wanted to die in the mountains!"

"You're awful!" she replied, as though the mere memory of the incident frightened her. "Why bring up that ancient history? You've coarsened over the years."

95

ALONG THE SHORE of Shinobazu pond, which seemed exhausted by the day's crowds and heat, the temporary shops and stalls were closing, but still people filed past in a steady stream. Individuals gathered around the phonograph in one of the eating stalls overlooking the water, and the man in charge was drinking sake and engaging in vulgar conversation with his women employees. Oshima heard the laughter and voices of wanton women and men who were passing by in search of secret pleasures in dark realms.

Oshima walked through the area as if she were in a sad dream. The exhibition's decorative electric light illumination had been turned off, and only the weird blue light of an advertising tower stood out against the gathering dusk.

She knew that news of the innkeeper's illness had cast a shadow across her heart. Her own world seemed suddenly emptier. But she also realized that she did not care as much for the man as she thought she did while away from him. Memories of her days in the mountains, before she even knew Onoda, produced only a vague longing. Her foolish, youthful love affair now seemed like crimson dye growing ever more diluted and blurred in water.

At the foot of the Kangetsu bridge, Oshima chanced to meet her young workman and Junkichi, an apprentice whom she was particularly fond of. The pair had left the gas burners of the hot workshop and were strolling around the town to take in the cool night air.

"How's the old man from the provinces—drunk again tonight?" Oshima asked Junkichi.

The two grinned broadly.

"Yes, he came home in good humor," Junkichi replied.

From Junkichi, Oshima occasionally heard how Onoda's father complained behind her back about the way she managed the house, but she paid little attention.

"Of course he'd speak poorly of me. A peasant like him couldn't begin to understand all I've built up with my own hands," Oshima declared with a laugh, but she was angry and offended that a newcomer to her household would look on her as just an ordinary housewife.

"I've received good news this evening, so I'll treat you both," she said.

"Thank you!"

"Follow me." She led the way, searching for someplace serving food.

"The old man told Onoda to divorce you," Junkichi informed Oshima over ice cream and cold fruit in a small shop open to the cool breeze off the pond.

"The fool actually said that, huh?" Oshima reddened in embarrassment. "Well, I regret to inform him that this wife isn't a meek little woman who's going to be put out of her own house by a father-in-law!"

96

ALMOST DAILY, Oshima was called out by her friends from the mountains to enjoy shows at theaters or vaudeville halls or to take gay day trips to famous historical sites in Kamakura and Enoshima. Before returning to Shiobara, the group came to say farewell to Oshima and Onoda at the tailor shop, and all departed but the master of the Hamaya, who stayed on for over a month, commuting to the hospital from a rented room that Oshima had found for him.

Oshima boasted to Onoda that her friends from the mountains were wealthy. When they came crowding into the shop—the innkeeper did not accompany them on this trip—she took them to the stifling room upstairs and served beer and chilled fruit. Onoda believed Oshima's story that she could extract capital investment from the group, so he came up and treated the guests with great politeness and deference.

The ever-practical Oshima did not neglect to obtain orders for fine clothing, such as a summer Inverness and a winter cloak. The miller promised that, if she brought her sample book to the town in the mountains, he would introduce her to many new customers.

"I can't tell you how much those gentlemen have helped me," she told Onoda after the visitors had gone, but even the slow-witted Onoda could imagine erotic episodes in Oshima's past from the familiar way in which the men spoke with her.

Onoda suspected that the miller, with rings gleaming on his plump fingers, was Oshima's patron in the mountains, and, after the departure of the visitors, he questioned Oshima.

"Rubbish," Oshima replied, blushing as she tidied the room. She had recently begun to have her full, black hair done in a fashion that particularly suited her, and, since the arrival of the guests, she had taken special care with her makeup. Among her many acquaintances was a jeweler, and she borrowed and wore new rings that Onoda had never seen before. In Onoda's eyes, all this made Oshima appear beautiful, an object worthy of his jealousy.

"If you weren't involved with him, why did you complain about my father going up to welcome them?" he asked, bringing up her conduct when she had the old man hustled off into a room where he would not be seen.

"But I'd have been embarrassed. He's your father, I know, but we couldn't have our guests see him. He'd have done your reputation more harm than mine," she argued.

"You were keeping up appearances for your former patron," Onoda accused.

"Have you no character at all?" she asked, grinning scornfully. "Those people'd simply laugh at you. If you think I'm lying, ask them. You'll only make a fool of yourself."

"Even if he wasn't your lover, there's still no excuse for making such a fuss over them."

"Oh, won't you just shut up!" Oshima finally shouted in impatience.

97

BY THE TIME the Hamaya's master, unable to endure the heat of Tokyo, returned to the mountains, Oshima had visited his room a number of times, and she could not keep these meetings altogether secret from Onoda. When the couple was short a little money, Oshima laid a loan from the innkeeper out in front of Onoda. She could not resist hinting that the man from whom she had borrowed the money was almost always amenable to her suggestions.

The innkeeper continued his trips to the hospital, but he tired of the injections—he had received about ten—and there were personal affairs that he had to take care of before midsummer. In the course of Oshima's many visits, he had discovered that her domestic situation with Onoda was not as idyllic as it appeared. He was concerned about her complaints, but he did not feel there was anything he could do to help her.

"Be patient, and don't use such extreme language," he cautioned in reply to one of her bitter recriminations.

On the verge of placing her head on his shoulder, she had been carried away by one of her stories about herself, saying things not truly in her heart, but, even though he listened intently, his perfunctory responses, always accompanied by a laugh or a smile, struck her as inadequate.

"You're a completely different person from the days in the mountains," Oshima said to him.

"I'm not the only one who has changed," he replied. As Oshima met his gaze, she felt shame at having her role as a wife seen through.

"I suppose in time we all change." Oshima sat up prim and straight beside the tired man, who was reclining on his lap robe, but she was too restless to stay and make polite conversation now that the pleasure and excitement had passed.

A lightbulb cast a weak glow in the upstairs room of the house in Nezu. As she had returned through the bustling streets cooled by an evening breeze, Oshima realized that she and the innkeeper were no longer perfectly suited to each other. Her heart was heavy, and she hesitated before entering the shop.

"I'd better meet this person," Onoda declared, intending to express his gratitude after Oshima presented him with the money.

"You mustn't! He's extremely shy. I wonder how such a gentle person's survived in the provinces, and he hates meeting people."

This seemed to satisfy Onoda, but he wanted to hear more about the fellow.

"He's better looking than most men in Tokyo," Oshima replied with a laugh, and she felt a blush spread across her face.

98

ON AN AFTERNOON shortly before the Festival of Souls, Oshima saw the innkeeper off at Ueno station, which was crowded with people seeking to flee the heat of Tokyo. With the departure of this last guest, Oshima and Onoda became aware that their business was again on the verge of disintegration.

Dressed casually in the sandals that Oshima had bought him, with his panama hat tilted over his forehead and carrying the various gifts he had Oshima purchase for his friends and family, the innkeeper boarded the train. Her hair freshly done, Oshima was wearing an expensive coat of crepe silk gauze.

They wandered in and out between the waiting room and the noisy lobby, which was filled with the ringing of hundreds of wooden

geta. The mood of the station brought tears to Oshima's eyes, causing her to remember her past life in the mountains.

"Westerners are so daring and energetic, don't you think?" she
exclaimed as a beautiful foreign couple passed in front of them, perhaps on their way to Nikkō. Oshima's voice was full of admiration, as
if trying to dispel the sadness of parting.

"Why don't you come with me?" the innkeeper proposed.

His skin, white as porcelain, had been slightly tanned by the sun,
and his eyes were more piercing. Oshima was dazed by the image of
herself traveling as the wife of the man beside her.

Even after he boarded the train, she continued her animated
conversation with him through an open window in the passenger car.

"When business picks up, come and see me at the hot spring,"
he told her, leaning out the window as the train pulled away from the
platform.

As Oshima trudged out of the station, her eyelashes were still wet
with tears. Her lingering affection for the man seemed to tug at her
heart.

During the Festival of Souls, Oshima was busy every day paying
debts and making the rounds of her customers to deliver orders. She
often forgot the master of the Hamaya, who had sent her a postcard
shortly after he arrived in Shiobara, but she was more certain than
ever that her married life with Onoda was not a happy one. She con-
templated her situation from time to time, though she was frightened that Onoda might perceive her true feelings. Oshima was careful to hide the shameful secret of her love affair.

The Tokyo Exhibition of Commerce and Industry concluded
during the hottest part of the summer, and stillness came to the surrounding neighborhoods like the sea recedes from the shore at low
tide. Until then, Oshima and Onoda were able to evade the reality
that their business was failing, but now the disintegration was palpa-
ble.

In her mad rush to raise money for the shop, she seemed to pass
daily through Ueno park, where the exhibition buildings were being
pulled down. In frustration, she wanted to abandon the shop, which
she was certain they would lose anyway.

"Bad luck clings to this place. We're going to start over in a new
location," Oshima recklessly declared to the wool broker, who was
still awaiting payment for the large quantity of cloth he had advanced
to the couple.

99

AFTER SEVERAL YEARS, the name of the fourth business that Oshima and Onoda established became widely known. It grew to be a substantial tailor shop replete with Western-style furnishings and a large stock of wool cloth piled on the shelves, but, when they first moved to this new location on the main commercial avenue of Hongō ward, the couple did not have the money to put one decoration in the bare shop.

This time, Oshima avoided the carpenter from Atago and hired one from a different quarter of the city, but she and Onoda did not have enough to pay for even one plank of wood for the flooring and shelves. Oshima, however, was roused by the challenge and fascination of creating something new, and this enabled her to call forth a resiliency in critical situations.

Oshima remembered an apprentice carpenter who worked for her father, and she went to offer him the job, which she represented as remodeling to accommodate an expanding business.

"Do you want me to provide the materials and save you the trouble?" the carpenter asked with a knowing look.

"Yes, please. We don't have time to find the best deals," Oshima replied.

The carpenters carted in the wood. "You see, it's easy," Oshima commented to Onoda. They still did not have enough money for the nails, but Oshima knew how to deal with the local hardware dealer.

"We're doing some construction in the neighborhood, and I'll be coming in here all the time to buy materials before it's finished. It'd be a bother to pay for each little item, so please open a line of credit for us. I'll leave this much as a deposit," she declared, convincing the shopkeeper.

The money for the deposit was part of the sum that she had received from a pawnshop the evening before for her bedding, which she had bundled onto the back of her apprentice, Junkichi, as soon as the sky started to darken. That bedding, made of silk, was the much-used last possession that Oshima had managed to hold on to since her days with Tsuru.

"Sink or swim, I'm staking everything on this last bet," Oshima declared dramatically as she sent Junkichi on his way bearing the yellowish-green bundle on his back. "If you do your work with the same attitude, I'll owe you a debt of gratitude I'll never forget," she added. Almost in tears, she watched the departing Junkichi, who struck her as a vulnerable youth.

"You have to train workmen from an early age. We can at least protect Junkichi from the influence of transient workmen. We must closely supervise the boy," Oshima commented in a low voice to Onoda, who was watching the carpenter.

With the help of two apprentices, the carpenter was busily measuring and sawing pieces of wood at the front of the shop.

100

WHEN THE CARPENTERS were almost finished, Onoda sent Oshima to the glazier they knew in the Nezu district to obtain glass for the showcase window and the door.

Oshima spent the morning going around to her customers boasting of her new shop, and she returned home at three with only a few repairs and no new orders, a result natural enough in the summertime.

The full heat of the yellow August sun seemed to penetrate the earth. She left the shop at about the time the cicadas were chirping in the trees, but, at every house she visited, she discovered that her customers had no money on hand or were away on vacation. At the home of a family she had known for many years, Oshima helped nurse a sick child for three hours, changing ice and cooling her with a fan. On her return to the shop, she was dizzy with hunger.

Inside, the carpenter and his apprentices were taking naps. Onoda was asleep in front of an open window, taking advantage of a refreshing breeze.

Oshima slammed drawers noisily as she changed into dry clothing. She was all the more exasperated by the fact that Onoda's father, whom they had sent back to the provinces when they left Nezu, had not settled his account at the neighborhood sake shop. On the street, Oshima had run into one of the clerks from the shop and was obliged to greet him first, demonstrating that she was not trying to escape the debt. If Onoda had not invited his father to Tokyo, they might have kept their shop in Nezu. The senile drunk had caused her so much worry he had been a major distraction from her business.

"Beating the old man to a pulp would be too good for him!" Hatred for her father-in-law still blazed within her. His drunken insistence that Onoda divorce her had caused no end of problems for Onoda and resulted in the domestic discord that finally forced the father to return home. Even Onoda's sleeping face enraged her.

"Wake up and get to work! You look stupid when you're asleep," she exclaimed in irritation when Onoda opened his eyes slightly and focused on her.

By the time Onoda had sluggishly risen to his feet, Oshima was already eating in the kitchen.

"Work, work, work. You're such a bitch, but there's no work to do," Onoda said as he smoked by the brazier. His bloodshot eyes looked tired from lack of sleep. "The most important thing now is the glass. What about that? We can't keep anything in the shop without it."

"Don't ask me! Why don't you come up with a few ideas for a change?" Oshima replied.

101

ONODA LOOKED AROUND the room. Oshima's sweaty under-robes were scattered about where she had dropped them. The drawers of her chests were a chaotic mess in the wake of her search for a change of clothing. He remembered his father's warning that Oshima would never learn to keep house, words spoken as he urged his son to divorce her.

He recalled his father's honest-looking face as the old man, shocked by Oshima's rough manner, cautioned, "She may have abilities in her trade, but otherwise she's a terrible creature. I can't believe she's a woman!"

"She leaves in the morning, and she's gone all day. What takes up so much of her time?" his father had wondered on another occasion.

According to Oshima, it was hard to work up enthusiasm for the day's business if she had to worry about making breakfast for everyone in the morning. And the day seemed pointless if she was not welcomed home by satisfied employees. So Onoda and Junkichi lit the clay charcoal cooking stove and kept the pickle barrels. Oshima enjoyed going out to obtain orders, but, when it came time for the customer to pay, Onoda frequently had to collect what was owed.

In the evening, Oshima regained her good humor and went to visit the glazier.

"Once construction on the shop's finished and we've built up a little capital, I'll have some flashy new flyers printed up and distributed. By the end of summer, we'll try to get into the market for middle school uniforms." Onoda told Oshima his simple, practical plan on her return.

"And your part in this," he continued, "will be to dress up in Western-style women's clothing and make the rounds of the schools to promote us and get new orders."

"No, the plan won't work. How much profit do you think there is in a school uniform?" Oshima argued, thinking that dealing in such petty seasonal articles would reflect poorly on her reputation. But Onoda insisted that, for a small-time operation like their own, without a splendid shop or large amounts of capital to attract upscale patrons, the only way to succeed was numbers and a high turnover.

Oshima knew that students were certain customers. She imagined herself dressed in Western-style clothing and mingling with groups of young male students. This image held a strange fascination for her.

"You'll become a famous person among the students," Onoda asserted, like a cheap theatrical promoter who has hit on a scheme and knows how to persuade his wife and daughters. Onoda's eyes gleamed with confidence that he could incite Oshima, thirsting for success and fame, to do his bidding.

Oshima felt that Onoda had defined the role she had been vaguely yearning for. She thought him clever and worthy of her trust.

"Sounds like a winner!" she concluded approvingly.

102

IT REQUIRED A CONSIDERABLE amount of time for Oshima to raise the money to buy a complete set of clothing from a Western-style dressmaker she knew in Yokohama.

In the window of the newly refurbished shop, Onoda hung a suit of formal court dress, light gleaming from its gold braids. He had bought the suit secondhand in the used-clothing district of Yanagi-wara.

The son of a glazier from whom Oshima had bought a full-length mirror installed the glass in the shop. The father had refused Oshima's appeal for credit; the son, who had heard of Oshima before, readily agreed.

"My father has his opinion, but I'm going to bet on your business instincts. I'll lend you as much glass as you need. If you fail, that's it; I'll write you off."

The next morning, the young man arrived with an apprentice, and they cut glass and put it in the show window and the front door.

"You're very intelligent for your age. Treat all your customers like you've treated me, and you'll be everyone's favorite. I'm personally going to introduce a number of paying customers to your shop," Oshima said, praising the young man as she sent him home.

The sign painter came to paint the shop's signboard, and Onoda raced around on his bicycle collecting samples of wool. Finally, the sample book, illustrating various styles of clothing, was hung in the shop.

It was well after the opening of the shop that Oshima wore for the first time a white summer dress and a large straw bonnet with a light blue ribbon around its high crown as she made the rounds of her customers.

"How do I look?" Oshima asked as she stepped away from her full-length mirror and came over to stand before Onoda and the workman Kimura, who had been employed by them again. The corset binding her substantial torso was so painfully tight that she could scarcely breathe. To cover blemishes on her skin, she had applied a thick coat of white makeup, and her face was ghastly and beautifully pale.

"You look ridiculously young. Some people might think you're a real foreigner. At least you'll pass for a Japanese magician just back from Hawai'i or somewhere," Kimura commented, laughing.

On her way to take orders from a dentist and a lawyer, two long-standing customers, Oshima met a group of students whom she was acquainted with.

"Here we thought it was a Western beauty from a foreign land, and all the while it was you!" one exclaimed, his eyes wide in amazement at Oshima's strange appearance.

"Come to our school in that getup," said another, and he stepped forward and shook Oshima's soft hand.

"The clothes were a huge success," Oshima declared on her return that evening. She immediately had Onoda help her out of the tight corset. When it was off, Oshima felt that her plump pinkish body had at last been restored to her.

Onoda had spent the whole day struggling over the design for the flyers that he intended to distribute to matriculating students at schools throughout the city.

103

STUFFING THE PRINTED FLYERS, each folded double and containing a schedule of the school's classes as well as an advertisement for the shop, into a woolen bag, Oshima set off early in the morning to stand in front of the gate leading to classrooms where first-year students gathered.

"Please take as many as you want and pass them on," she repeated as she distributed the flyers.

"We have a special agreement with a wool wholesaler and can bring you the latest styles at the lowest possible prices. Order your uniforms from us, and we'll give you a discount and do all within our power to make each of you a satisfied customer." As Oshima went on like this, she attracted a crowd of amused young people around her.

"These are cheap prices!"

"I understand she's a tailor just back from the West." Such were the whispered comments that passed between the students.

"Hey! Stop! You can't advertise here. Our school has contracted with other tailors," a gatekeeper or janitor would come tell Oshima, trying to chase her away because her flyers were littering the school grounds.

On occasion, Oshima took a few bills from her pocket and pressed them into the men's hands. She also did not neglect to win over the school's administrators.

"If the product's of high quality and you discount the price for our students, I don't suppose it matters where it's made. You're free to solicit the students if you wish," one administrator told Oshima, giving tacit permission for her to enter the school.

Wearing her Western-style dress, Oshima would appear among groups of students on the broad playing field.

At times she hired a ricksha to dash from one school to another, joining the gathering members of her trade. How she delighted in testing herself against this intense competition!

While Onoda and the employees were sleeping, Oshima left her bed and went to her mirror to apply her makeup. She then nimbly got into her corset and put on the petticoats, which she had finally grown used to. The ways the dress bit into her skin and the corset tightly squeezed her ample flesh gave her pleasurable sensations. When she slipped the high-heeled shoes on her tiny, graceful feet, a marvelous vitality came to her limbs; her stride seemed as light as air. She felt not the least shame or hesitation in leaping into places and situations she would never have dreamed of entering dressed in heavy, dragging Japanese robes and wearing the cumbersome traditional hairstyle.

On waking in the morning, her listless body craved the buoyancy provided by Western-style clothing. Dressing seemed to invigorate her wonderfully. If she did not appear wearing Western-style clothing on the dew-covered street early in the morning, the rest of her day was ruined.

Once Onoda, pushing a bicycle loaded with deliveries, drew up alongside her.

"It's a pity you're so short," he declared, staring at Oshima's full figure.

"These are my work clothes. I'm not concerned about how I look," Oshima replied.

The two walked together talking for a time.

104

In September, the flyers that the couple distributed began to show conspicuous results, and orders for winter school uniforms or overcoats with attached hoods flooded in. They increased the number of workmen in their shop. Dissatisfied with the slow progress that she made on foot, Oshima learned to ride a bicycle.

In the evenings, Oshima and Onoda, wheeling the woman's bicycle they had bought on an installment plan from a neighborhood shop, walked a quarter mile to a vacant lot, and, under Onoda's tutelage, Oshima practiced riding her bicycle. The bonnet she had worn daily for over a month was faded by the sun and its ribbon soiled with dust. In the gathering dusk, her round shoulders hunched up against her bonnet, Oshima practiced steering the bicycle, with Onoda at her side for support.

Paulownia and acacia trees on the vacant lot, on which a house was soon to be built, provided shade, and summer grasses grew in abundance. Recently constructed houses rose around the open ground. Circling the lot again and again until darkness descended, Oshima's white-clad figure attracted the attention of passersby.

Leaning her bicycle against a tree, Oshima crouched in the shade, resting her tired body. The hem of her skirt and her stockings were damp. Insects chirped in the grass.

Oshima cooled her perspiring body in the breeze, took off her wilting bonnet, and, slightly fatigued, listened with pleasure to the rhythm of her strong heart pounding. She felt a dull pain in her hips and buttocks. Onoda expressed the fear that riding the bicycle might damage her sexual parts, but Oshima's vision of herself racing through the city on the bicycle left her disinclined to entertain such doubts.

"So what if it hurts a little? I don't mind. We must do something novel, or a woman won't succeed in a man's trade," she said, grasping the handlebars again.

Oshima soon grew skilled enough to ride to the lot and practice by herself. Early in the morning, she would ride around and around in the shadows of the trees, mist striking her face. Autumn-like breezes lifted her skirt, and the tall grass, white with dew, bent to the ground. The faces of women or students gaped in amazement over the fences of the surrounding houses. Children on the embankment threw stones that fell in the grass.

"That's awfully tiring," Oshima told Onoda after she had put the bike away. She had been practicing for about a month and had just finished her first ride to Ginza, where she picked up material for the shop.

"From Suda-chō on, even I was frightened. Don't worry, though. I'll get the hang of it after a few trips," she said confidently.

105

IN FEBRUARY, after busy winter days that Oshima spent almost entirely on her bicycle, a lull came in the couple's business. Oshima finally had an opportunity to be examined by a doctor concerning her misgivings about her body. She had been too embarrassed to have it done before.

"All the hair's worn off, so the bicycle must be harmful," she told Onoda, lifting the skirt of her kimono to show him, but the injury appeared external and superficial.

Oshima's friend, the wife of a local dentist, had been admitted to the hospital for an operation, and Oshima visited her to wish her a speedy recovery.

Hoping to promote her business, Oshima was generous in tipping the nurses and orderlies, who immediately became her friends. She also became friends with several young doctors after they had examined her a few times.

The dentist's wife once worked in the demimonde and had sufficiently recovered from her illness that she had begun to regain weight. Oshima would place her gift of flowers in a vase and spend half the day in the hospital, talking and arranging the woman's thinning hair.

"I wonder if my body's normal?" In the presence of the nurses, Oshima asked her friend the same question she had once asked the mistress of the printing shop. "The union of husband and wife only gives me pain. It has no other meaning!"

"You must be doing something wrong," the patient replied, turning her radiant smile on Oshima. Color had returned to the woman's wan face, leaving it tinged with red and beautiful.

"I don't know, but I don't think so," Oshima replied, blushing. "This may be revealing intimate personal secrets, but I think he's the odd one!"

"Yes, perhaps one in a thousand men is like that," the young doctor who examined her replied with a chuckle in answer to the question that continued to bother Oshima. Oshima was already commuting to the hospital for treatments because a part of her body was said to be slightly out of place.

"You shouldn't put pressure on it, so stop riding the bicycle for a time," she was told during her first, painful treatment, and after that she dressed in Japanese-style clothing when she went out.

During the long period required for Oshima's treatment, Onoda spent much of his time bicycling around the city.

At the house of a customer, Onoda became acquainted with a woman who taught Japanese flower arrangement, and the tailor shop was now prosperous enough for him to hire her and purchase a phonograph as well. The web of the shop's borrowings and lendings had become so complicated that the uninformed Oshima could not quite comprehend the situation. But she herself was acquiring gaudy kimonos, and, cheerfully expecting new happiness in life, she daily passed through the main gate of the hospital for her treatments.

106

When Onoda was not making the rounds of customers, he generally remained at his cutting table. At the slightest interruption in the flow of work, however, he went over to fiddle with his phonograph. Oshima often discovered Onoda dozing when she had assumed he was listening, enraptured, to popular ballads.

Onoda had hired the flower-arrangement teacher for Oshima's cultural edification since she was now entering the homes of better families. Oshima ignored the woman and never took one lesson. She occasionally found the woman upstairs instructing the clumsy Onoda how to cut and place flowers in a vase.

The woman, who had an unhappy past as a man's mistress, sometimes stayed for several hours with Onoda. She spoke in the gentle manner of Osaka women, and this appealed to Onoda, a native of Nagoya.

"Even I have the impulse to insert the blossom first." Oshima heard the middle-aged woman's alluring voice make this suggestive remark as she climbed the stairs on her return from the hospital. A spasm of jealousy gripped Oshima's heart.

As the woman was leaving, Oshima confronted her at the entrance.

"I'm sorry, but I'm afraid we don't have the leisure for flower arranging. Please make this the last day you come," Oshima said politely, doing her best to keep her strained nerves under control. She offered the woman, who was in her late thirties, a parting gift of money.

Perfectly applied light makeup covered small wrinkles on the woman's coarse face, and she was dressed in an old-fashioned coat. She was frightened by Oshima's manner and departed with her head hung dejectedly.

"You stupid bastard!" Oshima yelled, scampering upstairs to confront Onoda. Not pausing to take off her coat with its huge family crest, her dark black hair now done majestically full, Oshima stood glowering down at the hapless Onoda.

"Growing a mustache and turning spoony over a woman like that, you really are a fool!" she declared, and, picking up the discarded stalks of cut flowers, she slammed them across Onoda's face. Her eyes were red and full of tears.

Enraged, Onoda threw the water pitcher at Oshima, leaving her sleeves dripping wet.

Not to be beaten, Oshima tipped over the freshly created flower arrangement, crushed and tore the flowers, and threw them at Onoda.

There was a fierce physical struggle. Oshima finally surrendered, and Onoda loosened his powerful grip on her neck. Her hair was a mess. The fight had left them exhausted, seated facing each other in opposite corners of the room.

107

THE COUPLE DESCENDED at about the time the lights came on in their shop and throughout the city. Since she had begun receiving treatments at the hospital, Oshima had concluded that Onoda's desire was a fearsome thing, and she kept her distance from her husband. This time, as well, they had parted with the usual sense of physical frustration and disappointment.

"Please find yourself another woman!" she exclaimed to Onoda, and even considered bringing back the woman who was introduced to him by the mistress of the printing shop.

"If I don't set him up with someone, I won't be able to continue in this business," she concluded.

Onoda's woman from their Nezu days, reputed to be of relatively good birth, had visited the Hongō shop a few times. Oshima had gotten rid of her by finding her a husband, a worker in an armaments factory, and acting as the intermediary for their marriage.

Oshima sensed that Onoda remembered the woman fondly and was visiting her in her room behind a shop in an alley in the Tozaki district of Koishikawa ward.

"What happened to that woman?" Oshima asked Onoda.

At the time of the wedding, she had been apprenticed to a restaurant and was forced to keep up her appearance, but, having married, she had let herself go.

"You may still feel affection for her, but the situation's different now. What'll you do if the wronged husband comes storming in here?" she said, reproaching Onoda for his inability to forget the woman, but she also thought it strange that the woman continued to feel attracted to Onoda.

"Her husband isn't that sort of man. He knows about our affair and doesn't care," Onoda replied with a smile.

Oshima had begun riding her bicycle again several days before, and, on returning one evening at nine, she learned that Onoda had been called away by a woman.

"Where'd he go?" Oshima asked, taking Junkichi aside. She knew that the young apprentice was aware of everything that happened in the shop.

"A young guy came from the Hakusan pleasure quarter. I took the letter he brought into Onoda myself, so there's no mistake," he replied, gazing at Oshima, who had not changed out of her Western-style dress. He watched her turning pale with anger.

"Then he's having a secret rendezvous there. I'll nip this in the bud!" she declared, and, hurriedly taking off her corset and slipping on Japanese-style clothing, she bolted out of the house. She remembered a restaurant where he occasionally went to drink.

108

THE WOMAN WHOM Oshima discovered meeting in secret with Onoda began to go mad after her confrontation with Oshima, and almost every evening she shouted and wept in front of Oshima's shop.

When Oshima came bursting into the room, the woman fled by way of the corridor, and, on seeing the terrifying Oshima chasing her up the stairs, she thought that she would be murdered and ran out into the night.

"Ungrateful son of a bitch," Oshima screamed at Onoda on returning to the room. Her pounding blood gave her a bestial strength that not even Onoda could restrain.

The small second-floor room where she found the two was red under the hot gas lights, and the smell of warm sake and the sounds of sweet whispering had further stimulated Oshima's rage. The woman's white rubber comb caught Oshima's attention and incited her violent impulses. Oshima and Onoda left the restaurant together, a light spring rain brushing their faces. Both had wounds on their hands.

On a spring evening while people were still abroad, the woman came to the front of the tailor shop and threw pebbles against the show window. She opened the door with a distracted smile on her pale, hysterical face.

"Is the woman of the house in?" she asked the apprentice as she glanced apprehensively toward the rear of the shop.

"Let me speak to your boss!" she demanded.

The apprentice merely smirked.

"He's out now. You'd better go home to your husband and rest," Oshima said gently. She put money into the woman's small hand. Grinning, the woman stared down at the currency and shoved it back at Oshima.

"I didn't come for money," she said. "I want to talk to your husband."

Driven from the shop, the woman wandered back and forth on the street muttering complaints as she waited for Onoda's return.

"If he has his accusations, I suppose we have our grievances against him," Oshima replied to the dissipated, fortyish man who pushed his way in and declared that he had been sent by the woman's husband. As their conversation progressed, Oshima frequently mentioned her uncle, once famous in the underworld. This caused the man to leave off his threats. It turned out that the visitor owed her uncle a debt of gratitude, and, in the end, Oshima won him over.

109

THE FILIAL ONODA left for the provinces to visit his father, whom he had not seen since the old man was sent home after the shop in Nezu failed. Onoda also wanted to show off his phonograph, still a miraculous new invention in rural areas. But, before he left, the couple had hired a young tailor whose skills were such that Onoda would not be missed during his trip.

In April, Oshima and Onoda had received a mass of orders for spring clothing, and Oshima had recruited the young man through a workman she knew. She was growing dissatisfied with Onoda's technique and appreciated the new tailor from the first day she saw him work.

The new employee had owned a shop, but he dissolved the business when he separated from the woman he had been living with. Leaving his household, he fell once again into the gangs of employed workmen. As a rule, refusing to put his shears to cloth of poor quality, he produced clothing that had a high reputation among the customers. Oshima often went over to the young man and watched his skilled, deliberate manner of working. His mastery of his craft prevented him from keeping up with rush or mass orders. Through this slender man, who had experienced so much for one so young, Oshima and Onoda were introduced to a world they never knew existed. Oshima was attracted to stories of the young man's amorous adventures, which he told over sake with his new friend Onoda.

"These jobs are a waste of my ability," he declared, refusing the work. No matter how busy the shop, the new workman would not consent to produce inferior garments.

"Then I guess you'll go on being poor," Oshima replied, but it pained her to supply the frail young man with such crude work. "Your refined tastes will be your downfall!"

As Oshima sat next to the young man, listening to his charming voice, she felt herself blushing to her earlobes. A small tattoo, little larger than a mole, aroused an odd desire to learn of the woman whose hand he held as the needle pierced his flesh.

"How old were you?" she asked, her eyes opening wide with a salacious glint when she discovered the tattoo.

"About sixteen," he replied, grinning broadly.

"What happened to the girl?"

"She's probably still in Osaka somewhere. I'd forgotten about her until you reminded me." He had sold the young woman into the corruption of the demimonde when he was pressed for funds at the end of the year.

"You hard-hearted men are despicable," Oshima said, laughing, but the histories of the various women he had so easily discarded held a strange fascination for her.

Leaving the side of the sleepy-eyed Onoda, who was changing records on his phonograph, Oshima approached the new tailor to hear more of his stories.

110

SOON AFTER ONODA LEFT for the provinces, Oshima suddenly felt the need to meet the innkeeper in Shiobara. Entrusting the shop to the new tailor, she set off for the mountains from Ueno station. It was a morning in early summer.

While receiving treatments at the hospital, Oshima became convinced that her body was not congenitally deformed, and, at the same time, she desired recompense for the suffering she had experienced with Onoda. Fantasies and desires welled up within her. She became more aware of the lack of sexual and emotional fulfillment in her life. The young workman's erotic stories aroused and made concrete her dissatisfaction.

The object of desire she pictured in her mind was invariably the innkeeper from the Hamaya.

"I'll go and see if I'm normal." Once Oshima made this decision, she wanted to visit her lover as soon as possible.

After the madwoman, who from time to time screamed abuse at the front of the shop, was committed to the public mental institution at Sugamo, Oshima felt free to depart on her journey to the mountains, the source of so many fond memories.

The woman, who had fallen into absolute nymphomania, became all the more insane once Onoda left for the provinces. Onoda's trip was in part intended to escape the madwoman. She had been discovered in the back of Oshima's shop trying to start a fire by lighting a pile of wood shavings and scraps collected from a nearby construction site.

The woman was arrested and led away by the police at the petition of the neighbors. Oshima witnessed one of the times the police strung the woman upside down from a beam in the police station and threw buckets of water in her face.

"You see! When we douse her with water, her eyes stay open. That's certain proof she's mad," the officer in charge said, laughing. They were in a room whose walls were lined with instruments of torture.

On the evening before she departed, Oshima served the new workman the sake he enjoyed, gave him money for living expenses, and asked that he look after the shop while she was away.

"I'm sure it won't happen, but, if my husband returns while I'm gone, make up an excuse for my absence. Tell him I've gone to pray at the grave of my former husband," she requested, reddening in embarrassment.

"Don't worry about a thing. Have a nice trip." The man smiled pleasantly, but his eyes narrowed in suspicion.

"To tell the truth, I have a lover," she could not resist confessing. "But you must keep that a secret from my husband."

111

OSHIMA, IN HASTE, departed from Ueno station at the beginning of June. She had purchased gifts and new clothing for herself to impress the people in the mountains, her guests during the Tokyo Exhibition of Commerce and Industry.

She could not discern in herself the feelings of five years before, the loneliness and despair that had made her vulnerable to her brother's persuasions. This time on board the train, her thoughts were of the thrill of tasting the fruit of forbidden pleasure.

The landscape of the Musashi plain inspired no memories of previous journeys. At large stations such as Ōmiya and Takasaki, Oshima leaned out the window to view her surroundings, but, having lived continuously in Tokyo for so many years, all the images seemed fresh and new. When she arrived at Takasaki, a number of happy-looking couples dressed in bright holiday garb got off to transfer, probably for the train to the resort area of Ikaho. She remembered Onoda, setting off with his phonograph to please his father. Laboring without rest throughout the year, dressing in those ill-fitting Western-style dresses, riding a bicycle—she was being worked to death for the benefit of a man who seemed to denigrate everything she did.

"I'm a fool to feel guilty about meeting the innkeeper! What's Onoda ever done for me!" she thought, and, in the train car, with no one to talk to, she pictured herself working so hard, without complaint, on the dirty streets of Tokyo. Selfish hostility toward Onoda led to the conclusion that he remained married to her for purely economic reasons. Doubts about the ultimate value of all her striving for so many years made her feel desolate and alone.

At some point, the train had left the green, fertile plain, blooming with the summer flowers of paulownia trees, and was climbing into the mountains. She noticed that the sun-streaked sky over Takasaki had been transformed by the rainy season's forbidding clouds. Precipitous mountains shrouded in gray mist rose outside her window. Huge drops of water splashed down from clouds floating over mixed stands of trees and grassy cliffs. Azaleas bloomed a brilliant red amid white boulders, as if from a brilliant scene painted on an old-fashioned folding screen. Water rushed down between craggy rocks.

Winding past a succession of high peaks and deep gorges, the train stopped at quiet stations perched on the high plain. The passengers stared in astonishment at the majestic mountains. Oshima grew more expectant and impatient at each station.

The train arrived in the vicinity of Shiobara at about four in the afternoon. Raindrops the size of rice husks clouded the windows of the car.

112

AT A SMALL STATION close to her destination, four new passengers boarded and took seats across the aisle from Oshima.

They seemed to have come from hot-spring resorts, for they were absorbed in conversation about people and events at such places even after the train started moving. Oshima caught fragments of their gossip about residents of Shiobara. She distinctly heard the name Hamaya repeated several times. A mountain that they strained to glimpse apparently caused them to mention her lover. The mountain, obscured by gray mist, was faintly visible in the distance, six or seven miles away.

"Excuse me, you seem to come from Shiobara. Has something happened to the owner of the Hamaya?" she asked, suddenly alarmed by what she had overheard. "I'm here from Tokyo because I have a little business with him, but, if I understand correctly, you were saying he had an accident on that mountain?"

The speakers, who appeared to be owners or patrons of establishments of the demimonde, fixed their eyes on Oshima.

One of them, his gold teeth glinting, recounted how the innkeeper had hiked up the mountain to inspect a tract of forest that he had purchased and, there, on a dangerous, narrow path in the rain, had slipped on the wet boards of a bridge and tumbled into the gorge. He was immediately carried down to the hospital, but his injuries proved fatal, and he died a short time later.

Oshima could not believe that the innkeeper had met such a miserable end, but, on inquiring further and learning the exact date and time of his death, she was gradually convinced.

"Then I suppose his soul was calling me here," she thought, and felt herself falling into despair.

Oshima arrived at the Hamaya in the evening, just as the rain was lifting. She noticed a few new houses built around the station square that she had once frequented, but, from the ricksha, it seemed nothing had changed on the main street. In her eyes, blurred by tears, the old town appeared to be stagnating in quiet solitude beneath the damp June sky.

That night she stayed in an upstairs room at the Hamaya, a room in which she had once worked at domestic chores, and the next morning she paid a visit to the innkeeper's grave at the cemetery on the outskirts of town. The innkeeper's family temple was at the top of a steep path climbing through close stands of tall pine and cedar trees.

The wind whistled through the pine trees as she left through the gate of the isolated mountain temple. Oshima could still hear the eerie sound of the innkeeper's tenacious gasping breath from beneath the grave. She hurried down the mountain path.

Oshima spent the morning at the Hamaya and boarded the train again at about noon. "I think I'll spend a few days at a hot-spring resort," she concluded. She had readily recovered from the despair that had gripped her heart.

113

SHE CHANGED TRAINS and then transferred to an electric tram, and early in the afternoon she arrived at a resort deep in the mountains.

The bathhouses were not yet congested with people. Most of the rental villas she saw from the street still had their gates locked. Heat from the June sun shimmered in a green dance across the pine trees. On the other side of the swift stream that flowed by the road, a moist wind blew through verdant grasses waving up the slope of the mountain.

Oshima was guided to a massive old-fashioned inn, and was given a room on the second floor with a magnificent view. The maid came to help her change into a cotton robe, and, as she was led down to the cavernous bath in the basement, Oshima felt the solitude of being the only guest at the resort.

Through the open window near the ceiling, Oshima noticed red clay crowded with grass roots that slowly dripped water into the bath. She heard small birds singing from the long, narrow pine branches that crisscrossed at the edge of the eaves.

Back in her room, a trifle fatigued from her bath, Oshima sat staring drowsily out the window.

"You must be lonely here all by yourself," the maid remarked as she brought in Oshima's dinner tray.

Oshima sadly considered the past two days of her trip and realized she had not once laughed out loud. The cheerful blaring of a phonograph came from one of the rooms.

Late that evening, Oshima went down to use the telephone. She called Tokyo to make certain that the shop was running smoothly in her absence. Onoda had not returned yet.

"That's perfect! While my husband's away, you can come here," she told the new workman, after she had instructed him to collect enough money for a four- or five-day stay. "And bring Junkichi with you. We've worked him hard for so long. The boy deserves a little vacation."

Oshima did not sleep well that night because of the sound of flowing water.

She woke at dawn anticipating the arrival of her visitors from Tokyo. For half the day, she waited in growing boredom and impatience. Her guests were shown to Oshima's room by the maid late in the afternoon, and they crowded in bearing baskets of fruit, changes of clothing for Oshima, and other luggage. The room suddenly became cheerful and animated.

"I know I'm here for hot-spring treatments for my health, but it's no fun all by myself," Oshima proclaimed in a gay mood to the workman, dressed in his finest clothes, and Junkichi, who was growing more apprehensive over Oshima's licentious behavior.

"Don't worry! I'll just tell Onoda the doctor prescribed hot-spring baths. That'll take care of his objections," she reassured the nervous apprentice. "Besides, I might leave that shop and set up my own business. We'll rely on the skills of our new tailor here," she continued. Oshima was hinting at a plan that had recently begun taking shape in her mind.

Appendix A
Chronology of Events

1884 Oshima is born to a prosperous family of landscape gardeners/village headmen in the Ōji region, now a part of Tokyo. Soon after her birth, she is sent to live with close relatives.

1890 After suffering terrible abuse from her mother, Oshima is led by her father to the bank of the Sumida river. It is intimated that he may have intended to drown her. By chance, her father meets a friend by the river. This man, Nishida, acts as an intermediary to adopt Oshima out to a nearby family of papermakers and moneylenders, the Mizushimas.

1900–1901 Oshima runs away from her foster family to avoid having to marry her foster father's nephew, Sakutarō, and she returns to the house of her true parents. She is persuaded to return to her foster family, but she is there tricked into marrying Sakutarō, and she runs away again the day after her wedding.

1902 Oshima is married to the widower Tsuru, a merchant specializing in canned goods, and she moves to his shop in the Kanda ward. The marriage is soon on shaky grounds owing to Tsuru's many affairs, his discovery that Oshima was once legally married to Sakutarō, and Oshima's jealousy toward Oyū, Tsuru's childhood friend and the present wife of Uegen's young master, Fusakichi. Toward the end of the year, Oshima returns to her natural parents' home in Ōji to give birth to Tsuru's child, but she suffers a miscarriage after her mother physically attacks her. With the loss of the child, her marriage to Tsuru ends in divorce.

1902–1903 Oshima is sent to work as a live-in servant at the house of Uegen, a family of gardeners who arranged her marriage to Tsuru.

1903 Late in the summer, Oshima accompanies her elder brother, Sōtarō, to the rural region of Shiobara in Tochigi prefecture to help him establish a nursery and gardening business. The business fails, and Sōtarō absconds, leaving Oshima as security for his debts. Oshima falls into an affair with the young master of the local inn, Hamaya.

173

1904 In the summer, fearing that his daughter has fallen into prostitution, Oshima's father comes and takes her home to Ōji. Oshima is then sent to live with an aunt who resides in Tokyo's Shitaya ward, and she works there as a seamstress. With the outbreak of the Russo-Japanese War, Oshima begins to do very profitable piecework for a tailor named Onoda. Onoda has a subcontract for the manufacture of warm winter uniforms for soldiers at the front. In December, at the height of the war-induced economic boom, Oshima forms a common-law marriage with Onoda, and together they open a tailor shop in the Tamachi district of the Shiba ward.

1905 By April, there ceases to be a demand for winter uniforms, and the tailor shop begins to fail. In the winter, Onoda and Oshima are forced out of their shop in Shiba, and they move to a smaller shop in a working-class neighborhood in the Tsukishima district of the Kyōbashi ward. On the verge of ruin, Oshima wins two hundred yen in a lottery, and the couple manages to pay off their debts by the New Year.

1906 In March, Oshima and Onoda liquidate their business and set off to make their fortunes in Shanghai. They travel first to Onoda's birthplace, Nagoya, where Onoda intends to raise money from his family for the journey overseas. The money is not forthcoming, however, and Oshima insists that Onoda return to Tokyo with her. They are employed for a brief time at a large tailor shop in Tokyo but are dismissed when Oshima refuses the sexual advances of the boss. In September, they find a small room to rent in the Atago district of the Shiba ward, and they begin taking orders for tailor-made Western-style men's clothing. Within five months, they have accumulated two thousand yen.

1907 In February, the couple rent a more spacious shop in the Nezu district of the Hongō ward, close to the 1907 Industry and Commerce Exhibition, one of a series of such exhibitions initiated by the national and local governments to stimulate the economy. They prosper during the exhibition, March–July 1907. Oshima is visited by her lover from Shiobara, who has come up to view the marvelous new technologies on display. With the closing of the exhibition in the summer, the neighborhood becomes once more a quiet residential area, and business falls off. Onoda and Oshima open a new shop on the main commercial street of Hongō. In the late summer, Oshima, dressed in Western-style women's clothing, begins distributing flyers advertising her shop's uniforms for middle school students. After a couple of months, at the start of the school year, this advertising has an effect, and the shop receives numerous new orders. Oshima learns to ride Onoda's bicycle, a daring move for a woman at the time. She takes to the bicycle so enthusiastically that the pubic hair around her genitalia is worn off.

1908–1910 The tailor shop prospers. Onoda has a love affair with a young woman. Enraged, Oshima breaks up the affair and drives the woman away. Onoda's lover later goes insane. In the spring, the couple hires an accomplished young tailor. Oshima is gradually attracted to this young man and his erotic stories. (This male character was modeled on Tokuda Shūsei's brother-in-law.) While Onoda is away in Nagoya visiting his father, Oshima departs for Shiobara to meet her lover, the innkeeper of the Hamaya. She discovers, however, that the young man has recently died in an accident in the mountains. Oshima feels that she has been summoned to Hamaya's grave by his soul, but she quickly recovers from her sense of loss and calls the young tailor to her side. She announces that she plans to break up with Onoda and set up a new business with her young employee.

Appendix B
Note on Japanese Words and Names

JAPANESE WORDS are romanized according to the modified Hepburn system used in the standard *Kenkyūsha New Japanese-English Dictionary*. Most of the unfamiliar references (e.g., *geta, obi, samisen*) can be found in *Webster's Tenth*. Two exceptions are *haori* and *hakama*. A *haori* is a Japanese half coat worn by men and women over a kimono. A *hakama* is a divided skirt for men, a pleated skirt for women, both worn as formal wear. "Dressed in *haori* and *hakama*," for example, indicates full formal dress.

Macrons are not used for well-known Japanese place names, for example, Tokyo. Names of Japanese persons are given in Japanese order, surname first.

In Japan, even today, although far less so than before the war, families and their individual members are referred to according to the name of the house (*yagō*) to which they belong. This is especially true in older, more established neighborhoods, where many families have the same surname. A stage name, the name of a profession, a name taken from a geographic characteristic or location, and the name of a business are some of the more common sources of derivation. In *Rough Living*, the most conspicuous examples of *yagō* are *Uegen* and *Hamaya*.

Uegen (lit. "source of flora") refers to the specific gardening business, the family that has operated it for generations, the physical house/business in the Kanda neighborhood, and individual members of the house, especially the head of the household. It may be a surname as well, but, if so, it was probably created as such in 1870 or later in response to an early Meiji edict requiring the registering of surnames with the government. *Hamaya* (lit. "house by the shore") is almost certainly not a surname. It refers to the business, an inn, the house the business occupies, the family that occupies the house, and individual members of the family, especially the head of the household.

Although it may be disconcerting to readers not familiar with the system, I have followed Shūsei's usage because the alternative would be to invent names with no actual textual basis or the frequent repetition of such clumsy circumlocutions as "the old woman who was the retired head of the household Uegen." A list of characters arranged according to family is provided in order to clear up any confusion.

177

Appendix C
List of Major Characters
Categorized by Family

Oshima's Natural Family at Ōji
Natural Father, head of a business/family of gardeners
Natural Mother, second wife who forms an irrational hatred for her daughter
Oshima
Sōtarō, eldest son of the family, declared mentally incompetent as a form of disinheritance
Oshima's older sister, wife of a former employee of the family business, friend
and confidant of Oshima's second husband, Tsuru, and his lover, Oyū

Oshima's Foster Family at Ogu, the Mizushimas (Surname)
Mizushima, foster father, papermaker and real estate speculator
Otora, foster mother
Mizushimas, Mizushima and Otora
Mizushima's deceased older brother, a criminal gang member, father of Sakutarō
Sakutarō, Mizushima's nephew, formally registered as Oshima's first husband

Family of Oshima's Second Husband, Tsuru (Given Name)
Tsuru, adopted head of a shop selling canned goods in Tokyo's Kanda ward
Kane, Tsuru's deceased wife, daughter of the founder of the shop in Kanda
Kane's half brother, owner of a shop dealing in canned goods in Yotsuya
The half brother's mother, probably a stepmother, a greedy woman whom
Tsuru despises

Uegen *(Yagō)*, House of Gardeners in Kanda Ward
Old Woman at Uegen, retired head/mistress of the family business, serves as an
intermediary for Oshima's marriage to Tsuru

Fusakichi, old woman's son, nominally the head of the Uegen family business but clearly under his mother's control

Suzu, Fusakichi's sister, whose husband is deceased

Oyū, Fusakichi's wife and Tsuru's lover

Hamaya *(Yagō)*, House of Innkeepers in Shiobara

Master of the Hamaya, called Hamaya when the reference is clear, Oshima's lover

Mother of the master, a widow and lover of the local rice miller who is financing the expansion of the inn

Wife of the master, living with her parents for most of the novel because of illness

Family of Oshima's Third Husband, Onoda (Surname)

Onoda, tailor from Nagoya with whom Oshima forms a common-law marriage and business

Onoda's father, alcoholic peasant

Onoda's mother, deceased

Onoda's sister, wife of minor bureaucrat in Nagoya

About the Translator

RICHARD TORRANCE is the author of *The Fiction of Tokuda Shūsei and the Emergence of Japan's New Middle Class* (1994) and a number of articles on modern Japanese literature. He is associate professor of Japanese at Ohio State University.